The Mystery of the Winged Lion

There were no gondolas available, so Nancy and George decided to take the *vaporettò*, the large water-bus that traveled up and down the canal.

The boat was already filled, but they managed to get on and squeeze through to the guard chain on the opposite side. They pressed close to it, watching the drops of sunlight on the small ripples as the *vaporetto* pulled away from the station.

Unexpectedly, a stranger stumbled roughly into Nancy, forcing her to move forward. Now she was poised at the very edge of the vessel with nothing but the chain between her and the water.

Suddenly the stranger thrust his hands onto her shoulders, pushing her down hard.

Nancy slipped and fell against the metal links, sliding under them before anyone could catch her!

Nancy Drew Mystery Stories

#57 The Triple Hoax
#58 The Flying Saucer Mystery
#59 The Secret in the Old Lace
#60 The Greek Symbol Mystery
#61 The Swami's Ring
#62 The Kachina Doll Mystery
#63 The Twin Dilemma
#64 Captive Witness
#65 Mystery of the Winged Lion
#66 Race Against Time
#67 The Sinister Omen
#68 The Elusive Heiress
#69 Clue in the Ancient Disguise
#70 The Broken Anchor
#71 The Silver Cobweb
#72 The Haunted Carousel
#73 Enemy Match
#74 The Mysterious Image
#75 The Emerald-eyed Cat Mystery
#76 The Eskimo's Secret
#77 The Bluebeard Room
#78 The Phantom of Venice
#79 The Double Horror of Fenley Place
#80 The Case of the Disappearing Diamonds
#81 The Mardi Gras Mystery
#82 The Clue in the Camera
#83 The Case of the Vanishing Veil
#84 The Joker's Revenge
#85 The Secret of Shady Glen
#86 The Mystery of Misty Canyon

NANCY DREW MYSTERY STORIES®

65

NANCY DREW®

MYSTERY OF THE WINGED LION

CAROLYN KEENE

PUBLISHED BY POCKET BOOKS

New York London Toronto Sydney Tokyo

This book is a work of fiction. Names, characters, places and incidents are either the product of the author's imagination or are used fictitiously. Any resemblance to actual events or locales or persons, living or dead, is entirely coincidental.

A Minstrel Book published by
POCKET BOOKS, a division of Simon & Schuster Inc.
1230 Avenue of the Americas, New York, NY 10020

Produced by Mega-Books of New York, Inc.

ISBN: 0-671-62681-7

First Minstrel Books printing January 1989

10 9 8 7 6 5 4 3 2 1

Printed in the U.S.A.

Contents

MYSTERY OF THE WINGED LION

1

Crash in the Night

"Isn't Venice romantic?" Bess Marvin sighed dreamily. Her eyes drifted from the hotel terrace where she and her cousin George Fayne were sitting to the moonlit canal that barely rippled under the oar of a passing gondola.

"Oh, it's okay," the pretty, dark-haired girl said, mildly enthusiastic.

"Is that all you can say?" Bess replied. "I'm sure if Burt were here, you'd feel different. I mean, just imagine if he and Dave were—"

"And don't forget Ned," Nancy Drew interrupted as she walked toward the table.

Ned Nickerson, Dave Evans, and Burt Eddleton were special friends of the girls.

"Nancy!" Bess exclaimed, a bit startled. "What happened to you? We were beginning to think you were kidnapped by the hotel concierge!"

Despite the smile the blond girl thought she would elicit, she noticed a grimness in Nancy's face that hadn't been there earlier when they arrived in Italy.

"Something's wrong, isn't it?" George said, making the same observation.

"I'm afraid so."

"Don't tell me there's a mystery in the Venetian air?" Bess put in. She rested her chin in one hand. "I mean, we *are* going to finish our vacation in peace, aren't we, Nancy? Please tell me we are."

"I wish I could," the young, titian-haired detective answered.

Her blue eyes traveled to the darkened windows of the great domed church across the Grand Canal, the largest course of water dividing the city. "If I live to be as old as that basilica, Santa Maria della Salute, I will never understand how this happened."

"How what happened? What are you trying to tell us?" Bess pressed the girl. Nancy drew in a deep breath.

"Ned, Burt, and Dave are in jail," she said.

"What?" her listeners cried aloud.

"Sh-sh. Keep your voices down," Nancy cautioned. "We just received a message—"

"From the boys?" Bess interrupted. "Where are they?"

"Here."

"Here—in Venice?"

"Let Nancy talk," George rebuked her cousin, but found it difficult to follow her own advice. "I thought they were flying directly back to New York after the Emerson College tour ended."

"That's what I thought," Nancy replied. "But now I have a hunch they were planning to surprise us."

"So they're in Venice!" Bess exclaimed.

She was ready to ask several more questions but Nancy quickly intervened. "The fact is I don't know any of the details—least of all, why they're in jail. Ned apparently phoned here. The message was brief and there was a phone number, which I tried calling. Unfortunately, I couldn't find anyone who spoke English.

"I finally asked the concierge to get on the line. He said something in Italian, mentioned Ned's name, and from that point on, all he kept saying was '*Si* . . . *si* . . . *si*.' When he hung up, he told me that the boys were in jail, and we would have to go there if we wanted to know more."

"Incredible," Bess said, pushing her chair back from the table.

"Where are you going?" George asked.

"To the jail, where else?"

"But it's after ten," Nancy said, "and according to the concierge, we must wait until morning when we can bring a suitable interpreter with us. He promised to get one."

"Gee, I hate to leave the guys stuck in that place overnight," Bess objected.

"We all do," George said, "but I doubt we could get them out without the help of a lawyer and maybe even the American Embassy."

Nancy now revealed that she had placed a telephone call to her father in River Heights. He was a distinguished attorney whose international connections might prove instrumental in freeing the three young collegians.

"There's a six-hour difference between Italy and the States," Nancy said, "so it's almost four-thirty at home. Dad's probably still in the office. At least, I hope so." She glanced at her watch. "Let's go back to our room. That call should be coming through soon."

Bess took one final glance at the glint of light dancing on the black water. It filtered out of several windows opposite the Gritti Palace Hotel where the girls were staying, including those of a large store displaying two fully lit crystal chandeliers and other glassware. Above the store was an elegant apartment framed in arches that curved roundly to an inverted V.

Suddenly, however, the chandeliers were turned off and there was a faint shatter of glass.

"One of the chandeliers must've fallen!" Bess cried out, causing Nancy and George to stop in their tracks.

"Well, I'm sure it didn't drop all by itself," Nancy said. "Maybe there's a thief in the store! Come on, we'd better investigate!"

"What about your father's phone call?" Bess asked as the young detective hurried ahead of her.

"I'll leave a message with the concierge to tell Dad I'll call him when we get back," Nancy said. After stopping in the hotel lobby for a moment, the three friends darted outside to the gondola station, where the gondoliers were talking animatedly. Apparently, they were unaware of what had happened across the way.

In the few Italian words she knew, Nancy persuaded one of them, a man with a full black beard and a deep crust of wrinkle over his eyes, to take her and the cousins to the other side of the canal. She told him what they had witnessed.

"Oh, I heard crash," the gondolier said in halting English. "But did not know where come from."

"The thief's probably gone by now," Bess announced as the boat pushed off.

"I'm not sure of that," Nancy said. "There's an awful lot of crystal in that place."

The ride took less than five minutes, and Nancy requested the gondolier to wait for them while they ran down the alley that led to the front entrance of the store. Upon reaching the building, they paused indecisively.

"There's nobody here now!" Bess whispered hoarsely.

"Sh!" George said, as footsteps sounded inside.

"He's coming out," Nancy murmured, pulling

her friends into an adjoining doorway.

"What if he's bigger than we are?" Bess went on, but neither of her friends answered.

The door was opening slowly, almost too slowly to suit Nancy. Then it closed again.

Oh, why doesn't the thief come out? Nancy wondered, her eyes suddenly lowering to the pavement.

The angle of a nearby street lamp had caught the girls' figures in its glow and threw their shadows in front of the store!

"Look!" she whispered to her friends, pointing to the shadows. "He's seen us."

"Let's get out of here," Bess pleaded.

"Just a minute," George said. "The door's opening again."

She felt the muscles in her throat tighten as the entrance remained ajar. No one emerged, however. Then, on impulse, Nancy surged forward, peering inside.

"Oh, Nancy, please don't," Bess begged as the young detective stepped into the store.

"Come on, there's no one here now," Nancy urged.

Reluctantly, Bess and George followed. They

tiptoed through one room into another, until they came to an open back door that led to the canal.

"He's gone!" Nancy exclaimed in disgust, staring at a speedboat that was just leaving.

"And we ought to go, too," Bess murmured.

Just then, as the boat passed the large window facing the canal, the intruder threw a heavy stone. It shattered the window instantly, setting off a shrill alarm.

"Come on, now we have to get out of here!" Nancy exclaimed, and rushed her friends to the front entrance. They ran into the street and down the alley into the waiting gondola.

"Hurry, please hurry!" Bess told the man.

The ear-piercing shrill of the alarm made him hesitate only a moment before he pushed off again across the black water. When they reached the dock, he helped the girls out of the boat, accepting several bills from Nancy.

"*Grazie*," she said, thanking him and darting toward the hotel without turning back to catch the look of puzzlement in the man's face.

To her dismay, there was no message from her father; and as they took the elevator upstairs, Bess added another note of concern.

"You realize, of course, that the gondolier thinks we broke into the store," she said.

"Well, we didn't," George said. "The door was wide open, if you remember."

"Try explaining that to the *polizia*," Nancy said. "I know we didn't do anything wrong, but somehow I do feel very guilty about it."

Once they were in their room, she swung back the shutters that overlooked the street entrance to the hotel. She saw their gondolier talking with someone who wore a hotel uniform, and motioned the cousins to the window.

Bess moaned. "He's probably turning us in."

"Maybe we ought to call the police before they do," George agreed.

"I suggest you learn a few words in Italian first," Nancy said. "Like 'I am not a thief.'"

"Very funny," Bess said.

"I'm dead serious," Nancy replied, as the jingle of the phone suddenly broke the conversation.

"There they are. The police. They've come to take us away." Bess groaned. "Well, at least the boys will have company in jail."

To Nancy's relief, however, the call was from

her father's office. "It's Dad," she announced happily, her expression quickly fading when his secretary spoke.

Miss Hanson explained that Mr. Drew had left town on business and was not expected back until the next evening.

"Oh, I see," Nancy said. "Well, would you please ask him to call us at the Gritti Palace Hotel in Venice as soon as you hear from him? Also, please call our housekeeper, Hannah Gruen, in case Dad checks in at home. It's very important."

"I'll be glad to, Nancy," the woman replied as the young detective said good-bye and hung up.

The girls spoke little while they readied for bed, taking turns in the shower and slipping into nightgowns before they slid under the covers. They had no sooner switched off the lamps, when a heavy rap on the door startled them.

"Don't answer it," Bess said fearfully, but Nancy had already turned the lights back on.

"What? And pretend we're not here?" George said, shaking her head. Nancy scrambled out of bed.

"Who's there?" she asked, throwing on a robe.

Surprisingly, no one answered but there was a second, more insistent knock.

"Who is it?" Nancy asked again. She stepped closer to the door.

This time a voice responded, but the words unraveled so quickly, the girl did not catch all of them. One, however, was painfully clear—*polizia*! The police!

2

Ned's Story

While Nancy reached for the door handle, Bess and George leaped out of bed and pulled on their robes.

"Oh, Nancy." Bess shivered nervously. She imagined that on the other side of the door was a big, burly police officer holding very large handcuffs.

To her amazement, though, it was only the night clerk. He smiled in a perfunctory manner.

"I am sorry to disturb you," he said in a heavy Italian accent, "but it seems that Andreoli, the gondolier—well, he told me you girls may be in some trouble."

He searched Nancy's face, then glanced at

the others, waiting patiently for an answer.

"You're right," Bess said impulsively, and felt a sharp nudge from her cousin.

"On the contrary," George said, "someone else is going to be in trouble as soon as we find out who he is."

"I'm sorry. I don't understand," the clerk replied.

"It's very simple," Nancy said and explained the details of what had just happened.

When she finished, the man released a long sigh. "I think perhaps it would be wiser if you told all of this to the police. Do you not agree?"

"Yes, I do. In fact, I plan to tell them everything tomorrow when we have an interpreter with us. The concierge said he would locate one to help us on another matter."

"I see. Very well, then. Good night."

As the clerk walked away, Nancy noticed that the bottoms of his pants legs were wet. Since it had not been raining, that seemed odd, and she mentioned her observation to the others.

"Maybe he fell into the canal." Bess giggled, feeling greatly relieved that her imaginary policeman had proved otherwise.

Nancy rolled her eyes in mock disgust. "Let's

go to sleep," she said. "Tomorrow's going to be a full day."

In the morning, the three girls awoke to a steady downbeat of rain. They dressed more warmly than usual, putting light slickers over their clothes, then headed for the terrace where they seated themselves under the protective tarpaulin cover. Immediately, they noticed the name of the glass showroom that bore a large crack in its front window.

"*Artistico Vetro*," Nancy said, translating the words. "Artistic glass. I wonder who owns it."

"Probably an old Venetian family," George replied, shifting her glance to the menu in front of her. "Prosciutto and melon. That sounds good."

Bess wrinkled her nose. "I'd rather have yogurt," she said, "with honey, of course."

"For a minute there, I thought you had finally decided to go on a diet!" her slim, athletic cousin teased, then turned to Nancy. "What about you? What are you going to have this fine, misty morning?"

"I don't know yet. I've been studying that store across the canal."

"Well, other than that hole in the window,"

Bess commented, "I don't see anything of interest."

"Even so, I'd still like to investigate further," Nancy countered.

"If you want my advice, I think we should stay as far away from that place as possible, especially since we're under suspicion for breaking into it!" Bess declared. "Besides, we have to see the boys."

"We have to do more than that," George said glumly. "We have to *free* them, and that's not going to be easy."

Nancy concurred with a deep, impatient sigh as their waiter handed her an envelope. She opened it hastily, then let out a cry of disappointment. The message inside had almost been entirely obliterated by the rain!

"I can barely read it." The girl detective moaned, passing it to her companions. "See if you can do any better."

But they were just as stymied. They hurried through the meal, finishing it with an inquiry.

"Who gave you this note?" Nancy asked the waiter.

"The concierge."

Questioning the concierge, however, provided no additional information.

"All I can tell you, Miss Drew, is that the envelope was here at the desk when I returned from the back office," he said. "Now let me introduce you to your interpreter."

He motioned to a young man who was seated on a bench opposite them.

"Antonio, these are the American ladies who require your assistance today," he said. "They need to go to the *Questura Centrale*."

"*Si*," the young man said with an engaging smile.

"Antonio is a student at the university," the concierge continued. "I think he will prove most helpful."

When the young man heard about the Emerson boys' predicament, he nodded sympathetically. "I will take you to police headquarters right away," he said. "Perhaps we can straighten things out. Follow me."

He led them out of the hotel and through a maze of small streets called *calli*, whisking the girls to the Rialto Bridge and finally, the police station. There in the lobby stood a high desk flanked by smaller tables. A captain in uniform looked up and greeted them very pleasantly in Italian.

Antonio spoke to him briefly, then the group

was ushered to a room at the end of a narrow corridor. Except for a table and a few chairs, it was empty.

"Please sit down," Antonio said, as the captain disappeared to get the prisoners.

None of the girls spoke, listening instead to the echo of their companion's foot tapping on the tile floor.

"How much longer do we have to wait?" Bess asked, but a minute later the Emerson students were brought into the room.

Instantly, it was filled with chatter and a deluge of questions from both sides that prompted the accompanying guard to clap his hands sternly. Antonio helped quiet the group, whispering to the officer who nodded back.

"You only have a little bit of time to talk," Antonio informed the Americans.

"In that case," Nancy said, "Ned, please repeat what you just told me. I especially want Antonio to hear this since he is going to help us get you out of here."

Ned, whose clothes were rumpled from sleeping in them all night, smiled gratefully at the young man. "If the police hadn't confiscated everything we brought with us, I could show you what they found," he said.

"Dave says you were stopped at Marco Polo Airport here in Venice," Bess interjected.

"That's right," Ned replied. "We stepped off the plane, went to the baggage area, picked up our luggage, and went to the customs officer. He made us open everything. That surprised me because I've always gone through foreign check-ins very quickly. Not this time, though.

"When the guy looked in my small suitcase, I almost flipped. There was the most beautiful glass artpiece inside—"

"What was it?" Bess interrupted, curiously.

"It was an abstract figure of a horse with hooves shod in gold. The customs officer started to examine it. He called somebody else over as well. I tried to tell them it wasn't mine, but nothing registered."

"The fact is," Dave said, "that neither of the men spoke much English."

"I told them I was traveling with friends," Ned said.

"And the minute he introduced us," Burt replied, "Dave and I were goners, too."

"Look, we'll figure out where that piece of glass came from," Bess declared, "and send it back where it belongs."

"That's just the problem," Nancy told her

friend, prompting Ned to finish his story.

"It broke into lots of little pieces," he said.

"What?" George gasped. "But how?"

"When the customs people kept turning it, it slipped through their hands—"

"And *splat*," Burt said.

"Oh, how terrible!" Bess cried, suddenly leaping out of her chair. "Well, then there's no case, no evidence, no nothing."

"On the contrary," Nancy said, "there's a lot of circumstantial evidence."

The guard who had been standing near the door now moved forward, signaling the end of the discussion. But before they left, the young detectives promised to do all they could to help the boys.

"Dad's due back this evening," Nancy said, "so I'm going to call home very soon."

"Sorry I messed up your trip," Ned answered bleakly.

"Don't be silly. I'm happy you're here—even if it is under lock and key!" There was a trace of laughter in her voice that barely masked her concern. "See you later," Nancy said.

When the girls reached the lobby again, she asked Antonio to request a look at the evidence.

He spoke to the police captain for a moment but to Nancy's chagrin, the officer was unwilling to show it to them.

"Tell him I'm a detective, Antonio," Nancy said.

"Your name?" the captain replied.

"Nancy Drew."

"Ah!" he said, adding something in Italian and finally the name of the Gritti Palace Hotel. Nancy also thought she heard him refer to the gondolier, Andreoli.

I should have told the police what happened at the glass showroom the minute we arrived here, Nancy chided herself. She watched the captain study her and the other girls closely.

"*Signorina,*" he said in a tone that forecast imminent doom, "I'm afraid you and these young ladies are also in trouble."

3

D. D. MYSTERY

The word "trouble" was enough to send Bess reeling.

"We haven't done anything wrong," she blurted out before anyone could stop her.

"Bess!" George hushed her, allowing Nancy to talk instead.

As concisely as possible, the girl detective told about the previous night's events. Antonio translated whenever necessary.

"I don't think the captain believes her," Bess whispered to her cousin.

"Listen, they're not going to throw us in jail," George said under her breath.

"Don't count on it. Especially when—uh-oh—wait till you see who's here."

"Who?" George asked, turning around sharply.

Amazingly, it was the gondolier who had ferried them across the canal the previous night. It seemed he had been summoned by the police to give an account of the girls' behavior.

We never should've run away like scared rabbits, Nancy thought, listening to the drone of the gondolier's words. He spoke in Italian, but too rapidly for her to understand everything. She looked questioningly at Antonio, who held up a hand to keep her quiet.

It was only when Andreoli finished talking that the girls' interpreter spoke. "The gondolier says you and the others insisted he take you to the glass shop last night," Antonio began.

"That's because we heard a crash and concluded there was a thief inside," Nancy said. "You see, the lights went out suddenly and we figured one of the chandeliers fell—"

Antonio smiled. "Andreoli says he heard the crash but did not know what happened because he was not looking in that direction. The police investigated and indeed, found a broken chandelier. They are still trying to discover whether anything is missing from the store."

"Then—they don't think we're thieves?" Bess stammered in relief.

"Are they going to let us go?" George added.

Antonio nodded. "But you must not leave Venice without telling the police, since the case has not been cleared up yet. Also, Captain Donatone says you must do no more investigating from now on. It will only get you into trouble. You understand?"

Bess giggled when they all left the police station. "You heard the man, Nancy. No more detective work. That means we're about to take an enforced vacation—a dream come true!"

"Oh, so you intend to leave poor Dave in jail!" George exclaimed.

"Hardly!" Bess grimaced. "But once the boys are out, we'll have no choice but to spend every moment lolling in the sun. Aah!"

"Well, it's still too early for me to call Dad," Nancy said, fumbling for the envelope in her pocket. "Antonio, I have something else to show you. Let's get out of this crowd first."

The rain had slackened to a fine drizzle, causing the girls to push back the hoods of their slickers as they cut away from the swarming tourists and headed for the Piazza San Marco.

"We'll have some cappuccino, if you like," their guide suggested.

"Oh, I like," Bess said gaily, following him to an empty table at Florian's.

It was one of several cafés where small orchestras played almost continuously in the shelter of the square's unending arcade, its stony gray facade now lightening under the passing raincloud.

Awestruck by the majesty of the cathedral opposite, Nancy temporarily forgot the reason she had hurried everyone away from police headquarters. The basilica, she concluded, was like a tapestry woven in mosaics and colored marble with figures of angels and saints standing guard over the huge gray domes.

"That was the church of the Doge, you know," the young man said, giving their order to the waiter. "He presided over the government of Venice—all one hundred seventeen islands that make up the city—and all official ceremonies were held there, not the least of which was the Doge's election."

As the observers noticed that only one of the famous *Quadriga*, the four stately bronze horses, remained above the central archway, George asked, "Where are the rest of the horses?"

"They are being restored," Antonio said, smiling. "After all, they've been here since the thirteenth century!"

Suddenly Nancy recalled Ned's description of the glass artpiece that had landed him in jail. It was an abstract horse shod in gold. Could it possibly be a modern version of this ancient statue? The idea penetrated her mind as Antonio continued to speak.

"It was the Doge—Enrico Dandolo, at the time—who brought the horses from Constantinople," he said. "To this day, though, nobody knows where they came from originally. Some believe Emperor Constantine took them from the Greek island, Chios. Others believe they used to decorate a Roman arch. But—"

"Yes?" George said as he hesitated.

"That's the mystery. Because, you see, no horses exist in Greek or Roman art that resemble our Venetian beauties."

"Speaking of mysteries," Nancy said, showing Antonio the message, "what do you make of this?"

He pondered it carefully while the waiter placed a cup of cappuccino in front of each person. The girls swallowed the frothy hot beverage in small sips, waiting for Antonio's reaction.

"Are you sure this was intended for you and not the police?" he asked.

"The envelope has my name on it," Nancy replied. "Why?"

"Well, because it seems to be a plea for help from someone who lives on the Grand Canal. That's about all I can make out, though. The person's name has all but washed away in the rain." He steadied his glance on the missing letters. "There is a capital *D* followed by a small *o* or *u*, I'm not sure which. Then, there is another capital *D* followed by a small *a*."

"Maybe it's from a *dogaressa*," George suggested, drawing a grin from the young man.

"I doubt it," he said. "They all died centuries ago. But it could be from a *duchessa* or a *duchessina*—"

"Who lives in a *palazzo*," Bess said eagerly. "Oh, Nancy, let's try to find her!"

"No police work, remember?" George needled back.

"Who says this is police work?" Her cousin chuckled. "If someone asks us for help, we can't very well deny it, can we?" She gulped the last bit of liquid out of her cup. "Come on, troops!"

"Unfortunately, I won't be able to go with you," Antonio said, "I have a class—a special summer course I just signed up for. But, please, if you need me later, call me. Here's my telephone number."

"You've already been a great help to us," Nancy said gratefully, promising to contact him if necessary.

Then, taking the lead, she and George left the café with Bess trailing behind. The latter had slipped under the arcade, pausing only a second in front of a shop window filled with glittering jewelry, much of it enamel.

But seeing her friends dart through the *sottoportego*, the passageway that ran beneath the buildings, she called out, "Hey, wait for me!"

"You must've found something you want to

buy," George said when her cousin caught up to them finally.

"I sure did. The most exquisite butterfly pin ever. You should see that place," Bess went on eagerly.

"Maybe tomorrow," Nancy said.

"I agree," George added. "We can't waste the afternoon shopping. There's too much to do."

Consequently, Bess carefully avoided looking in any other display windows along the streets that ran behind the square and the trio reached their hotel in less than five minutes.

"I hope Dad's home by now," Nancy remarked, putting the key in their door.

Her phone call proved fruitless, though. Hannah Gruen had not heard from Mr. Drew but she promised to have him return Nancy's call the minute he arrived.

"Thanks a lot," the girl said, and hung up the receiver in disappointment.

Then she hunted for the local telephone directory under the night table and scanned all the listings under D.

"Looking for a *duchessa*?" George inquired.

"No. Just someone whose initials are D. D.," Nancy replied. "After all, there's no reason to think the message came from royalty."

"That's true," Bess said, but a glance at the listings told her that if Nancy were right, the search could easily consume the rest of their stay in Venice.

Nancy came to the same conclusion and shut the book.

"No luck, huh?" George said, shifting some clothes out of her suitcase into an empty drawer.

The young detective did not answer. She was staring at the message again, concentrating hard on it, when suddenly a vivid image of the elegant apartment across the canal flashed into her mind.

Had the person who lived there seen her and her companions take the gondola back and forth from the Gritti? Had he or she somehow learned who they were and hoped to contact them?

Nancy mentioned the possibility to her roommates.

"Even though the police captain told us to stay away from *Artistico Vetro*, he didn't say anything about the occupants above it,' she added with a grin. "Also, I don't see why we can't inquire about other residents in the area while we're there."

Bess pinched her eyes in a tight frown. "I think that's asking for trouble," she said.

"Well, we'll go even if you don't want to," George declared.

"I wouldn't think of letting you go without me." Bess smiled.

When they went downstairs again, however, they were disappointed to find all of the gondolas had left the station.

"We'll have to take the *vaporetto*," Nancy said, referring to the large water-bus that traveled regularly up and down the canal.

She inquired about the nearest landing stage, then led the way through a small street that fed into a second one ending at the water's edge. The boat was already there filled with passengers, but the young detectives managed to get on and squeeze through to the guard chain on the opposite side.

They stood close to it, watching drops of sunlight on the small ripples as the *vaporetto* pulled away from the float, churning its engine loudly.

Unexpectedly, a stranger stumbled roughly

into Nancy, forcing her to move forward.

Now she was poised at the very edge of the vessel with nothing but the chain between her and the water. She tried to step back, but the crowd behind her would not budge.

Suddenly the stranger thrust his hands onto her shoulders, pushing her down hard. Nancy slipped and fell against the metal links, sliding under it before anyone could catch her!

4

The Duchessa's *Secret*

As Nancy slid forward, the passengers gasped in horror. Luckily, however, the girl had managed to grab the chain, keeping herself from falling into the canal!

"Nancy!" Bess cried, she and her cousin diving to help her. The stranger, meanwhile, had edged past them and lost himself in the crowd of onlookers.

"Just pull me," Nancy said hoarsely. "I can make it."

But her fingers were bone-white and threatening to give way any second.

"Lean back as far as you can," George told

her, putting her arms under Nancy's and tugging her upward.

"That's it. More, more," Bess urged. She watched the girl's feet grope for a toehold.

The ticket collector, who had been at one end of the *vaporetto*, now hurried forward muttering in Italian.

"*Che cosa sta succedendo qui*? What's going on here?" he asked as the young detective finally managed to swing her weight onto the boat and stood up.

"Someone pushed me," she said.

"*Non capisco. Che cosa dice*? I don't understand. What is she saying?" the young man replied. He looked at George for an explanation.

"My friend says someone pushed her," Bess answered. "Like this." She motioned with her hands. "You understand now?"

But the ticket man shook his head.

"Give up. Obviously, no one saw it because it's so crowded in here," Nancy said to the girls as the boat approached its first stop. She glanced through the passengers, most of whom where local people who spoke little or no English and quickly lost interest in the rescue once it was over. Which one of them, she wondered, had tried to push her overboard and why?

No answer came, though, as everyone hurried onto the landing stage.

"Do you suppose it was deliberate?" Bess asked Nancy after they debarked. "It seems to me there was very little standing room and someone could have bumped against you accidentally."

"It was deliberate all right," Nancy said, describing precisely what had happened.

"But who would want to hurt you?"

"And for what reason I'd like to know?" George added.

"That's what I keep saying to myself," Nancy remarked, as they ducked down an alley and walked to the *fondamenta,* the street that ran parallel with the canal.

When they reached the glass shop, however, they were surprised to find a sign on the door.

"'*Chiuso,*'" Nancy said. "How do you like that? It's closed."

She peered inside at the array of stemware glistening on the shelves that swept past elaborate mirrors to the chandeliers in the back.

Suddenly, Nancy's eyes fastened on someone's reflection in a mirror.

"Look!" she said, but Bess and George had already seen him. "It's Andreoli!"

Nancy tapped on the window, hoping the gondolier would respond, but he had already slipped out of sight.

"This is getting to be very frustrating," Bess said as an overhead window slid open.

"*Prego*. Can you come up?" A voice drifted down, causing the girls to step back from the building. The handsome elderly woman who had addressed them was probably in her seventies.

"Who are you?" Nancy asked.

"I will tell you when you come upstairs. There is a door to the right."

Without giving the girls another chance to speak, she closed the window.

"I wonder why she wants to see us," Bess said, following Nancy and her cousin to the second-floor apartment.

"She probably wants to kidnap us." George laughed, as the door swung open.

"Please come in, young ladies," the woman said graciously.

She gestured to a beautiful silk sofa that sprawled in front of a marble fireplace in the living room.

"I am the Duchessa Maria Dandolo. Perhaps you have heard of the Doge, Enrico Dandolo. I am a distant relative."

Nancy gulped excitedly, as she remembered Antonio's story about the Doge who had brought the bronze horses from Constantinople. "Did you, by any chance, send a message to me—Nancy Drew—this morning?" she asked.

"Yes, I did."

"But how did you know who Nancy was?" Bess inquired, incredulous.

"A friend of mine told me. Professor Bagley. He called to say hello before his college tour left Europe. When I told him I had a problem, he informed me that a very bright young detective was on her way to Venice. 'She's the person to help you,' he said."

"Oh, my goodness," Nancy responded, flattered by the professor's glowing recommendation.

"He also mentioned your friends, George Fayne and Bess Marvin," the woman continued, lighting her eyes on them. "He described you all so vividly that I immediately recognized you when I saw you standing downstairs. So . . . I take it you received my little note?"

"We did, but we could hardly read it," Nancy said. "It was washed out by the rain."

"Then, how did you know where to find me?"

"As you said, *Duchessa*, Nancy's a first-rate detective," George said, chuckling.

With that, there was a knock at the door, and the woman rose to answer it. To the girls' astonishment, it was Andreoli.

"You almost got us into a heap of trouble!" George accused him. "If you hadn't told the night clerk about our trip across the canal, we wouldn't have had to explain ourselves to the police, who, by the way, warned us not to do any more detective work!"

The gondolier looked crestfallen. "I not know who you were then," he said haltingly.

"Poor Andreoli. Don't be so hard on him," the *duchessa* said in his defense. "He told me about your conversation with Captain Donatone. I believe his restrictions concern only police matters. I am asking you as a private citizen to help me on a matter in which I do not wish to involve the authorities."

"Yes?" Nancy asked, her curiosity rising.

"I have a nephew who is quite brilliant, an artist like his father, and he—" She paused as if unsure whether to continue.

"And he?" George prompted her.

"Well, he has been kidnapped—taken away from Venice, his family, his work, everything."

"Why didn't you tell the police?" Bess asked.

"Because I did not want the publicity. If I reported the kidnapping, there would be stories in the newspaper. My family would be very upset."

Gazing at the elegant appointments in the room, the fine brocade, the crystal and marble, the girls concluded there was great wealth hidden between the lines of Maria Dandolo's story. Throughout, Andreoli had remained quiet.

"I want you to find my nephew," the woman went on. "I will pay you well."

"I never take money, and I am not sure I can accept the assignment anyway," Nancy said, surprising her companions.

"That's the first time I've ever heard Nancy

Drew turn down a chance to solve a mystery!" Bess exclaimed.

"Well, as Andreoli knows," the girl replied, "our friends are in trouble."

"They're in jail," George stated flatly.

"Yes, I know all about it," the *duchessa* said, "but what does that—"

"I'm afraid I have to devote my time to them until they are free. I'm sure you can understand that."

"Of course, but perhaps I can help you in that regard," Nancy's listener replied, causing a flutter of excitement among the girls. "I cannot promise, but I can certainly try."

She said something in Italian to Andreoli whose head bobbed up and down at every syllable. "*Si, si,*" he replied.

"But *signora*," Nancy started to say.

"*Duchessa*," the woman corrected her.

"Then, *duchessa*," Nancy continued, "please tell me how it is you can help my American friends when you fear going to the police about your own relative?"

"That is an easy question to answer. You see, I have many friends in high government positions who can—how you say—move things along for you. But Filippo. Well, he would be in even greater danger if I revealed his disappearance to them. I do not trust anyone now—except you."

The woman lowered her eyes, tracing a thin crack in a black marble table. "It's pathetic how old things break and fall apart with time," she said. "I'm trying hard not to let it happen to me, especially now. Please, you must find Filippo. It is your duty as a detective!"

5

Revelations

Nancy was thunderstruck by the woman's pronouncement and if it were not for her curiosity about the artist's disappearance, she might have politely excused herself.

The twinge of uncertainty in the girl's face was very evident. "Please, forgive me for talking as I do," the *duchessa* said softly. "I cannot force you to help me. I—I'm not myself these days."

"I understand," Nancy said. "Why don't you tell us more about Filippo. When was he kidnapped?"

"Less than three days ago while he was making some deliveries to our factory in Murano."

"Are his captors demanding money from you?" George asked.

"No. Not money."

"What do they want then?" Nancy asked.

Maria Dandolo gave a long, arduous sigh. "I cannot give you any more information until you say yes, you will help the Dandolo family."

"I will," Nancy said, "once the charges are dropped against my friends. They are completely innocent, you know."

"Fair enough," the *duchessa* said, smiling. "*Uno momento.*" She excused herself to a nearby telephone while Andreoli rose from his chair.

"*Scusi, signorine,*" he said. He spoke to the woman in Italian, nodded at the girls, and left immediately.

"Strange, very strange," Bess commented to her friends. "I mean what does a gondolier have to do with a duchess?"

"Maybe he's her private chauffeur or runs errands for her," Nancy said. "What intrigues me more is, what was he doing in the store below?"

When the woman finished making her call, she informed the young detectives of her success. It would take no more than two hours to clear the Emerson boys, she said. "You can pick them up about four o'clock," she added, sitting down again.

"Now I must confess something else to you," she continued. "I'm partly responsible for your friends' trouble.

"But how?" Bess asked, dumbfounded.

"My family has been in the glassmaking business for generations," the *duchessa* explained. "We own a factory in Murano and have several stores throughout Italy, including the one downstairs."

"Oh, then that explains why we saw Andreoli in the window before," Nancy interrupted.

The woman nodded. "Yes. He helps me with many things. But what I want to talk about is the particular glass sculpture that was found in Mr. Nickerson's luggage. It was one of the most beautiful things Filippo ever designed," she said sadly. "Ever since he was a small boy he's been fascinated by the *Quadriga*, the magnificent bronze horses atop the Basilica San Marco."

So I was right, Nancy thought. The glass statue was modeled after them! "Was Filippo carrying the piece when he was kidnapped?" she asked aloud.

"No. As a matter of fact, it had disappeared from our showroom in Murano a few days earlier. I reported the theft, and the police alerted customs officials throughout Europe to be on the lookout for it."

"So the chances are, if we find the thief, we may also find the person who framed Ned," George concluded.

"No doubt," the *duchessa* said. "I was afraid the sculpture would be taken out of the country, and apparently it was. But why it was planted in your friend's suitcase is still a mystery."

"Well, it's quite possible the burglary in your showroom last night was done by the same people who captured your nephew," Nancy offered. "What was actually stolen?"

"Nothing, or so it seems," the woman replied. "And the police have no idea why the chandelier fell. It is all so very strange."

She stood up and went to a writing desk from where she removed a piece of paper and handed it to Nancy. On it was a winged lion with a small Bible next to it and underneath, a few words in Italian. Translated, they said, "Peace to you, Saint Mark, my evangelist."

"Does this mean anything to you?" Nancy questioned.

"It does indeed. The winged lion and open Bible are the symbol of Venice. So are the words," Maria Dandolo answered. "Our patron saint is the Evangelist St. Mark. Filippo uses the symbol as a signature on his work."

"Then, are you saying that your nephew sent this to you?" Bess asked.

"Someone left it in my mailbox two days ago. You see, it has my address on the reverse side. Unfortunately, I don't know who brought it here. But it's unmistakably Filippo's handwriting."

"Perhaps he wasn't kidnapped," George spoke up. "Since no one has asked you for ransom, perhaps he just went away for a few days."

"No. There was a telephone call from someone—a man with a very deep, husky voice. He told me they had taken my nephew somewhere and said, 'You may not see him again unless—'"

"Unless what?" Nancy prompted her.

"'Unless you give us the formula that your brother, Filippo's father, uses to make glass with.'"

"Is Signore Dandolo the only one who has the formula?" Bess inquired.

"No, I think I have a copy somewhere among my papers."

"Why didn't they kidnap your brother?" Nancy volleyed another question.

"Apparently they couldn't find him at the time," the *duchessa* said. "So instead they took his most precious possession—his son."

"Where *is* Filippo's father?" the young detective asked.

"After my nephew's disappearance, he went into hiding, and I assure you, no one will ever find him."

The statement drew a long pause from the girls until Nancy spoke. "I see now why you don't want any unnecessary publicity," she said. "Not only because you might be risking further harm to your nephew, but also to his father. Have you no idea where they could have taken Filippo?"

"No, no idea at all." Maria Dandolo's eyes blinked sleepily as she finished speaking. "I am very tired now. I have not slept too well since all of this happened. Please forgive me. I must ask you to leave."

"We can talk later," Nancy said. "Perhaps we will have a chance to meet your brother as well."

"Perhaps. We will see."

In the meantime, Nancy and the cousins intended to contact police headquarters about the release of their friends.

"She seems to be holding something back from us," George said as they boarded the *vaporetto* for the return ride.

"She's just being cautious." Bess declared. "Don't you agree, Nancy?"

"I don't know quite what to think—yet. But I'm hoping the brains of Emerson College will come up with something."

"I'm sure they will!" Bess gleamed brightly. "Just think if we hadn't met the *duchessa*, Dave might have been forced to spend the rest of his days in a Venetian prison—"

"Pining away for his beloved Bess." Her cousin chortled.

"It isn't funny, George Fayne, is it, Nancy?" the girl said.

But the Drew girl wasn't paying much attention to the familiar, teasing banter between the two. She was thinking instead of the magnificent church built by the Doge Contarini for Venice's patron saint. It dominated the main piazza and its immensity was staggering. Undoubtedly there were numerous rooms inside and, behind the chapels, dark, unthought-of corners where someone could hide or be secreted away from the world.

Filippo's intriguing signature might, in fact, be a clue to his whereabouts! Nancy deduced. So the cathedral, the monument to the Evangelist Saint Mark, was the next logical place to search for the *duchessa*'s nephew.

6

Captured!

When the three girls finally debarked from the *vaporetto*, they returned to their hotel at once. To Nancy's disappointment, she discovered that she had missed the long-awaited call from her father by only a few minutes.

"I'd better try to reach him right away," she said. "I don't want him to worry."

So the instant the girls were in their room, Nancy dialed the operator who, unlike previous occasions, was able to place the call immediately.

"Dad, is that you?" Nancy said when the man's resonant hello crackled over the line.

"Nancy?"

"Yes, Dad. Oh, I'm so glad I finally got hold of you."

She explained the trouble that Ned and the other two boys had gotten into, quickly adding, "But we met a *duchessa*—"

"Who has connections in high places?" Mr. Drew chuckled.

"Exactly," Nancy said, smiling to herself.

She revealed the details of what had occurred, finishing in a cheerful tone. "So that's the story. No assignment for Dad this time!" she declared.

"Maybe you'll find one before I arrive, though," he replied.

"Before you arrive?" Nancy asked excitedly. "Are you coming to Italy?"

"Day after tomorrow. Believe me, it's as much a surprise to me as you. I have to help out a client in Rome. He was planning to consolidate his business with an Italian company that wants to expand to the States. But a problem came up, and I've been handling one end of it while his lawyer in Rome was supposedly taking care of the other."

"What do you mean 'supposedly'?" Nancy inquired.

"Well, it seems that the lawyer hasn't been pushing things along fast enough to suit my client. Anyway, I don't intend to spoil your fun with all of this dreary business."

"It's not dreary," Nancy insisted. "I just hope you find time to enjoy yourself while you're here. You are coming to Venice, aren't you?"

There was some hesitation in her father's voice before he answered. "If I can manage it—I'll call you as soon as I get into the hotel in Rome. I'll be staying at the Grand."

The conversation ended shortly, and Bess let out a long sigh. "I'm tired," she said.

"But it's not even three o'clock," George remarked, giving an involuntary yawn.

"See what I mean?" Bess said. She stretched out on the bed, shutting her eyes for a moment while Nancy spoke.

"It'll be another hour before we can pick up the boys at the police station," she said. "I'd like to visit the basilica on the way. Anybody want to join me?"

"Sure," George responded, but the gentle snore that dissolved in Bess's pillow proved she had already fallen fast asleep. "We can leave her a message."

"Good idea," Nancy said and scribbled something on a piece of hotel stationery. "I'll tell her to meet us in front of the central arch in forty-five minutes."

"What if she doesn't wake up in time?"

"Then we'll go on to headquarters without her."

Wasting no more discussion on the subject, the girls left the hotel for the piazza, which was now filled with pigeons and a long line of tourists in front of the basilica.

"It's really awesome," George said, following Nancy inside, and fastening her eyes on the colored mosaics and marble which were no less splendid than the arrangement of domes and arches.

Although Nancy had told George her idea that Filippo might be held captive in the building, both girls now tended to dismiss the idea, seeing the number of people who poured endlessly through the cathedral.

Nevertheless, they stayed in the line of visitors until they found themselves on the steps of the presbytery, the space around the main altar, gazing at a magnificent block of fine, hammered gold composed of enamels and precious stones.

"It's beautiful," Nancy murmured, pulling back to get a broad view of it along with several other visitors who were taking pictures.

George, at the same time, had moved down the marble steps, closer to the panel and away from Nancy. She was suddenly surprised when the young detective darted toward her and tugged on her arm urgently.

"Come on," Nancy said.

"What's the hurry?"

"I'll explain later."

But as the young detectives pushed their way to the far side of the cathedral, the twilight glow from the overhead windows was swept into darkness.

"Can't you tell me where we're going?" George asked her companion.

"I'm looking for someone—a man who came up behind me while I was standing at the altar. Unfortunately, he ran off toward the north transept. I didn't get a good look at him before he fled."

"Did he talk to you?" George asked.

"Yes. He—he—warned me to stay away from the Dandolo family. Otherwise—"

"Otherwise what?"

"He said I'd end up like the Doge Dandolo himself."

"He's buried in a crypt below here," George said, her throat catching on the words.

"I know."

"Maybe we ought to go back to the hotel."

"Are you kidding? No, sir."

Undaunted by the mysterious threat, Nancy pressed deeper into the arm of the transept, discovering a small, empty chapel at the end. The scent of burning tallow was unusually strong, suggesting that someone had recently doused candles near a door hidden in the shadows. Curious, the girls walked toward it, wondering whether the man had used it to escape.

For a fleeting moment, they imagined footsteps running in their direction and turned sharply. Then, unexpectedly, the door flung open and four strong arms reached out and grabbed them.

"Let g—" George cried, her words garbled

quickly by the hand that dragged her through the doorway.

Nancy also tried to shriek but to no avail as a gag was quickly drawn over her mouth and she was thrown face down alongside George on something soft and tufted like a quilt. The girls' wrists and ankles were tied next. Then the men left, closing the door after them and locking it.

Question after question tripped through Nancy's mind as she wondered who the men were and what they intended to do with their captives. Were they connected with Filippo's abduction? If so, might they not keep Nancy and George prisoners until they had finished with the Dandolo family?

We could be trapped here forever! Nancy concluded.

A similar fear had also occurred to George and she made a futile attempt to roll over but found herself pinned next to a wall. It felt cold and damp as her fingers brushed against a thin opening that seemed to run up and down in a straight line. George grunted into her gag, trying to tell Nancy she had discovered another door, maybe one that was unlocked!

Nancy understood instantly and looked up and down the crevice, searching for a doorknob but none was apparent in the darkness. So, with a hopeless sigh, she lay back on the blanket, breathing in its dank, musty odor.

Bess, on the other hand, had awakened out of her deep sleep and upon discovery of Nancy's message, she had quickly freshened up. She took the elevator to the lobby and strode toward the door, stopping midway when the night clerk greeted her.

"Where are you going in such a hurry?" he said, flashing a smile as he approached the girl. "You must slow down. Enjoy yourself." He added something in Italian that Bess did not understand.

"I have to meet my friends in front of St. Mark's," she told him.

"Well, perhaps I will go with you."

Bess looked at him quizzically and although she didn't wish to offend the man, she said abruptly, "I'm sure I can find the piazza without assistance."

"I'm sure you can, but I would like to come anyway. We go."

So rather than discuss it further and lose more time, Bess let him follow her outside.

"Shouldn't you be working?" she asked him.

"Not till later," he said. "Now tell me about you and your friends. Do you plan to stay in Venice a long time?"

"Not really. Just a week. Of course—"

"Of course, what?"

By now, the two had passed over a small bridge leading to a string of *calli* that fed into the square, and Bess tried to avoid giving an answer.

"Thank you very much for accompanying me," she said pleasantly, hoping at last to part company as the basilica loomed into view.

But the man pretended not to hear the remark and picked up his pace as they crossed under the arcade. When they reached the main portal of the church, however, Bess was disappointed to find her friends weren't there.

"I don't see them anywhere," she said anxiously.

"Perhaps they are inside."

"Perhaps," Bess replied. A glance at her watch told her she was only a few minutes late, so it was quite possible that the young detectives had not yet left for headquarters.

"Follow me, please," the man said in a tone of authority. "We'll find them."

"But—" Bess tried to protest, thinking she would miss the girls if they stepped outside while she went in. Even so, she tagged close to her guide, concluding that Nancy and George might, by chance, wait for her.

Once inside the building, however, Bess almost lost sight of the man as he dived between the huge marble columns leading to the north transept. Before taking another step, she glanced through the crowd, but not seeing Nancy or George, she darted ahead, following the clerk a few feet. Then she stopped, suddenly aware that he had drawn her away from the rest of the tourists.

Instinct told her to turn back, but the man's voice echoed out of the shadows, halting her.

"They're here," he called, and drew the unwitting girl forward.

7

Reverse Approach

Bess eased through the darkened chapel, which now carried only a faint scent of candles. "Where are you?" she asked, failing to conceal her nervousness.

"Over here."

But in the bleak emptiness of the room, the man's reply seemed to come from different directions.

"Where? I can't see you," Bess cried.

He struck a match and lit one of the candles, casting an eerie glow on the far door and sending a shiver of fear through Bess. She started to turn away, but it was too late. A thick, woven scarf billowed over her head and was pulled back tight between her lips, preventing her from screaming. She stumbled forward, trying to wrest herself from her attackers, but it was no use. They shoved her through the open door, and in her blindness, she tripped over her friends and fell between them, eliciting loud moans. Instantly, her wrists and ankles were tied like theirs. Then, the door clicked shut and the men departed.

Until that moment, Nancy and George had remained hopeful that Bess would be the one to rescue them. Somehow, though, she too had been tricked. Now they wondered if anyone, even the Emerson boys, would ever find them!

Despite the *duchessa's* promise, it was almost eight before Ned, Dave, and Burt were permitted to leave police headquarters. At the Gritti Palace, they registered and went to their room quickly, then dialed their friends on the next floor. To the boys' surprise, the girls weren't there.

"Very strange," Ned said. "I wonder why Nancy didn't leave a message for me."

"Maybe they got tied up somewhere," Burt answered, unaware of the truth in his comment.

"But it's so unlike her," the boy continued, feeling strangely uneasy. He spoke to the night clerk again. "Are you sure you have no idea where Miss Drew, Miss Fayne, and Miss Marvin went?" Ned inquired, observing beads of perspiration along the man's forehead.

"I'm quite sure, but—ah, come to think of it, they did mention going to the Lido."

"That's the beach." Dave laughed. "I doubt they'd get much of a tan in the Venetian moonlight."

"As a matter of fact—" The man bristled. "There is quite a bit of night life over there. Perhaps your friends found some charming escorts."

The remark nettled Dave since he was positive the girls would not succumb to casual dates with strangers. If anything, they were probably on the trail of a dangerous criminal!

"Listen," Ned went on, "how do we get to the Lido?"

"By the hotel boat. Or," he added quickly, "if you don't care to wait for the next one, which is due here in an hour, I can arrange for a water taxi."

The boys quickly looked at each other, agreeing to the latter suggestion immediately.

"Just go through that door," the clerk instructed, nodding past the newcomers. "And welcome again to the Gritti."

"Thanks," Ned said. He stepped outside, but realized a moment later that he had left his wallet in the boys' hotel room and excused himself. "Don't leave without me, okay?"

"Don't worry!" Dave and Burt called back as he darted into the lobby a second time.

Now asking for his room key once more, Ned flew to the elevator and took it one flight up to Room 124, but when he tried to open the door, it wouldn't budge. Again and again he jiggled the lock without success, then gave up and returned to the lobby only to discover that the clerk had left the desk unattended.

Now what? the boy wondered as a voice from behind pulled him toward an adjoining office. There, he found a man in a hotel blazer talking animatedly on the telephone. He glanced at Ned, but made no effort to end his conversation.

"Ned!" Dave shouted through the door off the landing-stage. "Taxi's waiting!"

"Okay, okay," his friend answered, dropping

the key on the front desk. "I just hope you guys have enough lira for all of us tonight."

He quickly explained what had transpired, causing Burt's and Dave's eyebrows to lift. "Maybe we'll wind up sleeping on some baroque sofa in the lounge," Burt groaned as the trio climbed into the boat.

Ned let the comment pass, speaking to the driver instead. "Lido," the boy said briefly just to confirm their destination.

"*Si. Capito*," the man replied, sending the boat through the inky-black water toward the lagoon where a cruise ship lay anchored in a brilliant dazzle of lights.

"I guess he understands," Dave commented, descending to the cabin below.

Ned and Burt, however, chose to remain outside. They were fascinated by the foamy trail of whitecaps that curled in the wake of their boat as it streaked along a channel of log markers flanking the course to the Lido. As it came into view, Burt pulled out a map of the beach resort, noting the main hotels offering musical entertainment. One of them was the Excelsior where they seemed to be heading.

"It sure is dark around here," Dave said,

sticking his head out of the cabin to feel the cool settling of air as the boat slackened its speed.

"I'll say," Burt remarked.

"And you and I had better duck before we get our heads knocked off by that bridge coming up," Ned told him.

The driver had already motioned them down. Keeping his eyes fixed straight ahead, he cut the engine and allowed the boat to glide slowly between the brick walls until it cleared the low, stony arch.

At the same time, Ned noticed the dark figure of a man on the other side of the bridge. He had lowered himself with a rope and was dangling to the right of the arch, holding himself with one hand while the other swung out, sending a small shapeless object in their direction.

"Watch out!" Ned cried to the boatman who instantly shifted the gear into reverse and stopped. The mysterious object fell a few yards short of its target and sank into the water.

"What was that?" Burt asked, mystified.

"Well, I don't think he would've climbed down a rope just to throw a stone at us," Ned said soberly.

"You're right. It was probably a bomb of some sort," Dave grumbled.

"Good thing it didn't hit the boat and go off. We'd be a plate of spaghetti by now," Burt said.

The driver, meanwhile, had continued backing away from the bridge, and Ned stepped quickly toward him. "We must keep going," he said. "*Prego*. Please. We have to go to the Hotel Excelsior!"

But the boatman shouted back in Italian, refusing to shift forward again.

"He's scared," Burt said. "He knows it was an attack, not just some kid's prank."

"At the rate we're going," Dave said, worried, "we might not get another taxi for hours. I think this calls for drastic measures."

"Like what?" the other boy replied, watching his friend's eyes travel to the murky, black water.

"I'll show him it's safe," Dave said, stripping down to his shorts. "Follow me!" he yelled to the helmsman.

"Dave? Are you crazy?" Ned called out but his words faded under the shouts of the driver, as the boy dived in.

"Now he's really in a tailspin," Burt whispered, watching the man angrily shift the boat forward.

"Have to admit it worked, though," Ned said.

Dave had succeeded in swimming several yards beyond them before the boat caught up to him, and he was reluctant to come aboard again. Apart from a possibly heated confrontation with the driver, he feared that the man might turn back. But the boys insisted that Dave had had enough exercise and pulled him out of the water.

The driver merely glared at him as Dave spoke, shivering, "It's freezing down there."

"Here. Dry yourself off, good buddy," Burt said and handed him a towel from the cabin.

"For this, you deserve a big dish of pasta on me!" Ned chuckled. "Too bad I don't have my wallet."

The remark drew a good-natured frown from his companion, who put his suit on quickly. "I can always take a raincheck," he said as the boat swung under a second bridge and finally pulled up to the hotel float.

He paid the driver, who offered a grim steely grunt in return, and then followed his friends into the hotel and down a long carpeted hallway. From the second floor, they heard a drumbeat and leaped up the stairway two steps at a time, hurrying past guests in glittering evening attire. The boys paused, however, when they reached the noisy room above.

"There she is! That's Nancy!" Dave gasped, directing Ned's attention to an attractive, titian-haired girl in a green silk dress. She moved off the dance floor with her date behind her and sat down at an empty table for six.

Soon a shock of wavy blond hair resembling Bess's also bobbed into view.

"See?" Burt said. "They did find dates and came here to dance."

"Hmph. It would serve them right if we left Italy without even telling them," Dave said, pursing his lips.

"I have a better idea," Burt replied, an air of mischief in his voice.

8

The Cap Clue

While the boys stood gaping at the crowd of dancers, Nancy, Bess, and George lay bound and gagged in their dark prison, their skin prickling with its damp chilliness. The hours had slipped away, and they wondered if their captors intended to abandon them forever!

I've got to get us out of here, Nancy said to herself, feeling the rope on her wrists cut deeper as she tried to work it loose.

Her companions shifted into slightly more comfortable positions: Bess sat against one wall and George leaned against the other with the mysterious opening in it. If only she could get to her feet to explore the rest of it!

She pressed her shoulders back and dug her toes into the floor beneath the blanket, pushing her weight upward. She made small progress before sliding down again, then repeated the exercise, getting no further than before.

Come on, George Fayne, where are those old judo muscles? she prodded herself.

She continued her attempts to stand up until the ache around her bound ankles became unbearable and she was forced to stop. Bess, on the other hand, had discovered a rough projection of wood at the base of the wall. She rubbed her wrist binding against it, snapping a few of the rope threads, and pressing hard to break the rest.

Although the girls' captors had buried them in impenetrable darkness, they hadn't taken away their ability to hear; and the sound of rope splitting over something sharp gave renewed hope for escape.

Nancy pulled herself next to George, groping for a nail or a piece of chipped wood, anything to help cut her bindings. George did the same but, finding nothing, determined to make one last attempt to get up.

She rapped her knuckles against the wall and hoped Nancy would understand that she needed her assistance.

She wants me to help anchor her, Nancy concluded, swinging her legs against George's feet.

That's it. Good, the other girl thought and pushed back and up again, allowing her toes to press into Nancy's tightening muscle. Inch by inch she moved until at last she felt a latch.

She's found something—a door handle perhaps! Nancy gasped excitedly. She dared not budge, however, waiting for the next signal.

George slid her body to one side and continued to hop back on her feet until she was able to stand, using the wall as her support. The latch, she soon discovered, was a few inches out of reach and she sighed unhappily. Nonetheless, the bindings on her ankles had loosened a little and she decided her exercise hadn't been entirely in vain.

Bess, meanwhile, had tired of her own labor and gave Nancy a turn at the piece of wood. The young detective ran her rope cuff over it in a sawing motion, stopping only once when a twinge of pain shot through her arm. No doubt she would find deep welts in her wrists she decided, but put the thought out of her mind as the rope started to snap. Just like Bess's, the threads broke a few at a time, then more, but the remaining ones were stubborn. They held fast like steel; and suddenly the young detective realized that only part of the cuff was rope. The rest was wire!

Now, for one of the few times in her life, Nancy felt beaten. She could never break wire over wood. She needed something stronger, like metal, and yet there was no way to communicate her discovery to George or Bess who had met the same obstacle.

Unaware of their friends' predicament, the Emerson boys had ventured across the dance floor at the Hotel Excelsior. Ned in particular kept his eyes on the table where the titian-haired girl had recently sat down.

"All set?" Burt asked his two companions.

He had noticed an attractive group of three girls, who seemed to be together, and walked toward them.

"American by any chance?" Burt inquired, drawing giggles from two of them.

"Not quite," the third one answered a bit disdainfully. "I'm from London, and they're from Austria."

"Well," Burt went on clearing his throat. "I'd like to introduce myself and my friends."

"We're very happy to meet you," the blondest girl replied. "My name is Helga Doleschal and this is Elke Schneider."

"I'm Christine Mott," the Londoner said.

As the boys told about their recent trip through Vienna, the conversation rippled with laughter until everyone rose to dance. Ned swung his partner toward the end of the room hoping to catch Nancy's eyes, but at the same instant, he realized that her table was now empty! He scanned the dancers, but she wasn't among them.

"Is something wrong?" Christine asked.

"Huh? Oh, no," Ned answered in the midst of his distraction. He wondered, though, how he and the other boys could have missed seeing Nancy and the cousins leave; and when the music finally stopped, he whispered to Burt and Dave.

"Obviously they're gone. Maybe we ought to go too," Ned said. "I'm bushed, anyway."

"Me too," Dave said. He muffled a yawn. "It's not everyday in the year I get to swim in a canal!"

"You—swim in canal?" Helga asked. "I did not think you were permitted to do such a thing."

"You're not," Burt laughed, "but he doesn't understand Italian warning signs."

"Tsk, tsk, tsk," the girl replied in mock disapproval. "Perhaps you will have to stay in Venice until you learn. We'll be here at least through Saturday."

"So if we need a few lessons in Italian, can we depend on you to teach us?" Dave grinned.

"*Senza dubbio*. By all means."

The young men offered a few more pleasantries, then waved good-bye, wondering if their American girl friends had already returned to the Gritti Palace. Considering the lateness of the hour, it seemed more than likely.

"Shall we call them when we get in?" Burt asked.

"Why not?" Dave said, while Ned reserved his answer until they were down the corridor.

"Actually, I'd like to check out that bridge," he said.

"The one where the bomb came from?" Dave replied.

"Yup."

"But I thought you were tired."

"Well, let's say the brisk night air just woke me up."

As a matter of fact, Ned had been itching to investigate the area but had decided not to until he had tracked down Nancy. Now he was ready to begin again, and led his two companions out of the hotel to the street.

He tore down a flight of steps and cut through clumps of oleander into an empty garden that trailed along the small canal.

"Suppose we get arrested for trespassing?" Dave asked Ned.

"Suppose we do?" Burt said. "It's better than being accused of theft."

Ned chuckled. "I hope you both realize you're beginning to make me feel guilty over absolutely nothing," he went on, and pushed beyond the dimness of a few lamp posts.

The threesome now walked evenly toward the bridge, looking for any evidence of the person who had thrown the explosive.

"I'm sure it was homemade," Ned murmured.

"Lucky for us it wasn't designed to go off in water," said Burt, when he spotted a dark felt cap on the ground.

He dived for it, noticing footprints as well. They were fairly small and close together, which implied they belonged to someone shorter than either of the boys.

"Let me see the cap," Ned requested, peering at a well-worn label inside. "Didn't we pass a store with this name?"

He held it in front of Dave and Burt.

"Yes, on the way to the Gritti, I think," Dave replied, "but there are probably hundreds of people who own hats like this one."

"And I'm sure the proprietor won't remember who bought it," Burt concurred.

"Even so, I'm going to hang onto it," Ned remarked. "One thing Nancy taught me is never take any clue for granted."

"I'm not convinced that bomb was strictly intended for us," Burt said.

"Well, if it wasn't, then who was it meant for?" Dave asked.

"Maybe our boat driver," Burt suggested.

"I doubt it," Ned said.

"But why would anybody want to hurt us?" Burt asked.

"I don't know," Dave replied. "Perhaps it's all tied in with the trouble over that glass statue."

"True," Ned said, "and I'd sure like to find out who masterminded *that* little frame-up."

"Wouldn't we all," Burt declared, as the putting sound of a boat approached from the hotel. "Uh-oh, I think we just missed our ride back."

He and Dave had observed the boat schedule on the canal entrance to the Excelsior, and cast frowns at each other.

"There'll be another one," Ned said confidently.

"No, there won't," Dave answered. "Not until tomorrow morning."

"Are you positive?"

"Positive."

"Oh, well, considering all that's happened tonight—" Ned sighed. "I guess we ought to be glad it isn't raining, too."

With that, a flash of lightning cracked through the sky and small bullets of water trickled down the boys' faces.

"See what I mean?" the Emerson boy said, tossing his shoulders in disgust. "That takes care of our detective work!"

9

Thwarted Search

As rain heaved itself in waves across the canal, Ned and the other boys ran back toward the hotel from where the last boat of the evening had just left. They tried to attract the driver's attention but it was no use. The rain was beating harder now and blurred their vision.

"Hurry," Ned said in a panting voice. "Maybe the guy at the dock can radio the boat back."

But when they reached the man in uniform, he was huddled behind the door talking to someone else.

"*Scusi,*" Burt said, attempting unsuccessfully to cut into the conversation. Dave cast an impatient glance at Ned who was equally dismayed.

At last, however, the man turned to them, and, hearing their predicament, said he would call a water-taxi as soon as the storm lifted.

"That could take hours," Dave said pessimistically.

"Boy, I hope not," Ned replied. "I'm exhausted—"

The rest of his comment faded quickly, though, as a young, titian-haired woman in a green silk dress trailed down the stairway carrying a large umbrella. She paused briefly at a display of clothing in a window, then turned, aware of Ned staring at her.

"Look," he whispered to his friends, "that's the girl we saw upstairs."

"And it isn't Nancy," Dave remarked sheepishly. "Now what?"

"Well, before we do anything else, let's call the Gritti and see if the girls are back."

"Good idea," Burt agreed, following the other two to the main lobby.

After a brief explanation to the concierge, Ned was offered the use of a nearby phone. The call went through immediately despite an interruption of static, but to his disappointment, the answer was the same as before. His American friends had not returned.

"Oh, but—yes—wait a moment," the night clerk said. "There is a message here for you. Shall I read it?"

"Yes, please," Ned answered, waiting anxiously while paper rustled out of an envelope at the other end.

"It says— Are you listening?" the clerk inquired.

"Yes, yes, I'm here," Ned said. "Go on."

"It says, 'Sorry we weren't able to see you today. Something unexpected came up and we had to leave Venice. We'll try to be back by tomorrow, but if we can't, we'll see you at home.' It is signed, 'Your friend, Nancy Drew.' "

"That's all?" Ned asked.

"*Si.*"

"Please put it in our box then," he said. "We'll pick it up when we return."

"As you wish."

With that, Ned hung up the receiver. He was troubled as well as mystified by the contents of the letter, which he related to Burt and Dave.

"It's not only the formality of the signature," he stated.

"You can say that again," Dave interposed. "At least, Bess would've signed 'Love, Bess.' I mean, does Nancy always add her last name?"

"No, never. But what bothers me more is the fact she didn't say where they all went."

"Obviously, they're on a secret mission," Burt concluded.

"Hmph. Since when is a secret mission a secret from us?" Dave answered, eliciting a nod from Burt.

"And what's all this business about seeing us at home if they don't get back to Venice?" Ned added in a tone of disbelief.

"That is a bit much," Burt agreed, "but I guess we'll have to take a look at the handwriting to make sure it's from Nancy—"

Another crash of thunder ended the discussion, however, and the threesome returned downstairs, determined to press the man on duty for a taxi. But he remained adamant.

"I am sorry," he said. "I cannot do anything for you. No one will come."

"But what if it was an emergency?" Dave asked.

"What can I say? Look at the rain now. It's worse than ever."

As he spoke, gusts of wind spilled angrily across the canal, churning the water into high waves.

"Too dangerous, too dangerous," the man repeated. "You sit, or go upstairs and dance. Enjoy yourselves—inside!"

If only the boys could, but they felt trapped and helpless, wondering where Nancy, Bess, and George had disappeared to.

The time passed slowly as the threesome wandered through the hotel again, looking in display windows that lined the corridors while hoping for a letup in the weather.

"Hey, check this out," Dave said, drawing his friends' attention.

"What is it?" Ned replied absently, then focused on a shelf of crystal. These things look very similar to the piece the customs man found in my suitcase!"

"Don't they, though?"

The boys noted the signature under the manufacturer's sign. It was an unusual design of the famed winged lion followed by the name Filippo.

"He sure makes some beautiful stuff," Burt commented, "and judging from the fact there aren't any prices on it, I bet it's pretty expensive, too."

Although they anticipated finding more samples of the artist's work, they didn't and finally gave up their search.

"I was just thinking," Dave said. "Suppose Nancy's note isn't legitimate? The night clerk told us they mentioned going to the Lido. What if they're still here?"

"Well, I'm sure they wouldn't have missed the last boat back to the Gritti," Burt said.

"Unless they did by accident or were forced to," Ned replied. "Weather permitting, we can still make a search of the beach and every hotel."

But there had only been a temporary break in the storm, which now grew stronger than ever.

"It looks as if we'll have to book ourselves in here for the night," Ned continued, "and postpone our investigation until tomorrow."

"That's fine with me," Burt said, glancing at Dave who nodded also.

Despite the fact that it was peak season at the beach hotel, the boys were able to obtain a room. It was considerably more expensive than they had counted on, but they took it anyway.

"What's a few lira more or less when our friends may be in danger?" Dave said as they registered their names.

"Exactly," Ned agreed. "But remember, I don't have a wallet."

The other boy smiled limply. "In that case—" he sighed—"I guess we'll have to settle for cold rolls in the morning."

"Could be worse," Burt said, as they followed the porter to the elevator and their room, which proved to be a small suite.

"Maybe we ought to stay up to really appreciate all this," Dave quipped, gazing at the velvet furnishings and tasseled drapes.

"You go right ahead," Burt said, "but I'm going to bed—immediately."

A deep yawn emphasized his intention.

"Me, too," Ned added, collapsing against his pillow. Dave followed suit, but only after one more sweeping glance.

With the steady downpour of rain thudding against the windows, he barely imagined next morning's sunlight.

But the next day, it burst across the boys in a blaze of warmth, jolting them awake.

"Close the drapes," Dave mumbled as he pulled the sheet over his head.

Ned had already dived into the shower, leaving Burt to pry Dave out of bed.

"Get up," he said. "It's after nine."

"Okay, okay," Dave answered but made no attempt to move.

"Don't you want to find Bess?" Burt went on, stretching to his full frame.

"Sure, sure. Just give me five more minutes."

However, by the time they all reached the dining room, it was well past ten o'clock. Ned had made one final call to the Gritti to see if there was any further message from Nancy; but as he suspected, there was none.

During the course of the night, the girl detectives had been carried to another room within the basilica. It had happened while they were sleeping. Their gags had been doused with something sweet, to assure their abductors there would be no struggle. When the prisoners awoke, they felt light-headed, aware of the sickening odor that still clung to their nostrils.

They must've drugged us, Nancy surmised. But why?

She stretched her legs out groping for the familiar wall but it wasn't there, and the young sleuth realized they had been moved. No doubt they had been secreted away in a room where there was no chance of anyone finding them!

Her only consolation, though, was that Ned and the other Emerson boys were probably out of jail by now.

When they don't find us at the hotel, they'll know something happened, Nancy thought, and they'll start searching right away!

10

Troublesome Discovery

Nancy's other hope was that her father would be arriving in Italy, too; and he would join in the search, unless, of course, he became immersed in his own case and did not try to call Nancy until later in the week!

As these troublesome thoughts continued to plague her mind, she dragged herself backward, bumping into George and Bess who also realized they were in a new location. They, like their companion, had begun to explore it. But Nancy was the first to discover an old radiator with a thin metal pipe that jutted out from the base.

She slipped her wire cuff over it and rubbed

back and forth until her bonds snapped in half, freeing her hands at long last! Then she reached for the gag around her mouth, removing it just as quickly.

"The wire's off," she told her friends happily, "and I'll get rid of the ankle rope any minute. Just be patient."

But her words fell short as footsteps in the distance echoed along the marble floor.

"Someone's coming. Uh-oh," she said, putting back her gag.

The footsteps stopped momentarily, and the young detective wondered if the person was one of their captors. But before she could think about it further, she heard men's voices, muttering Italian in low, growling tones. Still, Nancy understood a few of the words, among them the name Dandolo!

Filippo's kidnappers! she gasped. But what are they saying about him?

Instantly, she freed herself and her friends, signaling them to remain quiet as she peered through the door lock. But a lug was in it and she could not see the men.

"What if they find us like this?" Bess whispered nervously.

"Sh," George warned her. "Nancy's trying to listen."

But the girl detective was not having much success. She strained to hear the words passing between the two, catching only a few that made no sense to her at all.

"What are they saying?" Bess asked.

"Be-ess," George chided her again.

"I'm not sure. Something about 'Roma' and 'Murano,'" Nancy replied.

"Rome and Murano—hmph," George repeated. "I wonder—"

The sound of footsteps interrupted again, and Nancy slid away from the door.

"Quick! Put everything back on," she warned. Fast as lightning, the girls obeyed, holding their breath as the shuffle of feet stopped on the other side of the wall. The men spoke again, but in low, indistinct voices that faded as their steps unexpectedly changed direction.

"Whew!" Nancy sighed moments later when it was clear the men had left.

She tried pushing the lug out of the lock but it wouldn't give.

"Now what will we do?" Bess asked, showing the same fearful expression that usually drew a word of comfort from her friends.

This time, however, George said, "I'm not sure."

"Neither am I, but—" Nancy started to say.

"But what?"

"Well, it seems to me we have two choices. We can either wait here like three sitting ducks or try to get out."

"But we already tried," Bess countered.

"Oh, I know, but I have another idea."

While the young detective revealed her plan of escape, the Emerson boys were working on their own investigation. They had checked out of the Hotel Excelsior and walked up the beach, observing the long rows of cabanas that obscured their occupants from view.

"Maybe we ought to ask if the girls signed up for one," Ned suggested.

"Just lead the way," Burt said, leaping down the terrace steps to a small entranceway.

There they found several guests from the Gritti Palace who had arrived only minutes before. They were eagerly awaiting the cabana assignments listed on a large sheet of paper bearing columns of names.

"That's what we want to see," Dave whispered to his friends.

Although they were impatient, they waited politely for the other people to finish and leave, then made their inquiry. Unfortunately, it led to a negative response.

"Of course, they could be using a cabana at another hotel," Burt offered.

"Not if they're guests of the Gritti," Ned replied. "It has a reciprocal arrangement with the Excelsior regarding cabanas. Come on, let's go."

The boys continued their walk, pausing briefly to admire the deep azure water that lapped in gentle waves against the shoreline.

"It'd be nice just to lie out there and bake." Dave sighed, turning his face up to the sun.

"Okay, beach boy, that's all the tan you're going to get today," Burt teased, picking up his pace. "It's hard to believe there was a storm last night, isn't it?"

Upon closer observation, though, he realized it had done more than leaf damage to the trees. A telephone line had come down, along with a traffic light that lay splintered in the road.

"How far do you want to go?" Dave asked Ned.

"Just up to the Hotel Des Bains. I figure if the girls got stuck here overnight they'd probably want to get back to the Gritti to change, and they'd have to take the boat from the Excelsior."

"What if they were on the trail of something important?" Burt asked. "You still think they'd rush back to the Gritti?"

"Let's put it this way," Ned said. "We haven't passed them yet, so there's a chance we may."

But the trip to the Des Bains proved as fruitless as everything else, and the boys decided to take the next boat back to the Gritti. As soon as they arrived, they requested to see Nancy's message.

To their amazement, it wasn't in their mailbox.

"But the night clerk said he was going to leave it for us," Ned insisted.

"You will have to ask him, then," said the man behind the desk. "I know absolutely nothing about it."

"Well, perhaps you can send someone up to open the door to 124," the boy went on, glancing at the key in front of him. "This didn't work for me last evening."

A look of puzzlement greeted the statement. "Then how did you get in?" the man inquired.

"We didn't," Dave said. "We got stuck in the storm at the Lido."

"Oh, I see. Well, just a moment. Let me call someone to help you."

The clerk disappeared into a back office and a porter soon picked up the troublesome key. The boys followed him upstairs, and stood watching as he inserted it into the lock, turning it gently until it clicked open.

"Now how is that possible?" Ned said, utterly astonished, as the porter nodded and left. "Maybe I dreamed I—"

"Old cheapo here thought he'd save a few lira by leaving his wallet behind." Dave laughed teasingly.

"That's me, all right." Ned grinned and opened a dresser drawer, pulling out the wallet and a few coins inside. "Here you are."

"Huh?" the other boy replied in bewilderment. "I mean, what's this for?" he said, as Ned dropped the coins in his palm.

"I think it's important to keep one's reputation intact," the boy said briefly, allowing a long silence before he broke into laughter. "If you could only see the look on your face!"

"Mine?" Dave gulped, catching a glace in the mirror. "Hey, what's that?"

He pointed to a thin crack along the bottom of the glass.

"I wonder how that happened," Burt said. "It looks as if someone threw something at it."

"Like this, perhaps?" Ned said, holding up his penknife which he had picked up from the floor. "It was in the top drawer."

He pulled open the drawer, the contents of which were in complete disarray.

"Somebody's been in this room, all right!" Ned declared. "Check the other drawers and your luggage."

The boys wasted no time examining their things.

"All my stuff is here," Dave announced shortly.

"Mine too," Burt added.

"Well, I'm not missing anything either," Ned said, staring at the mirror crack. "It seems to me someone must've been awfully frustrated to do that—just because he didn't get what he was looking for."

"Maybe, or else he was in a big hurry. He started throwing things out of your drawer and the penknife hit the mirror."

"But if that's the case, then why isn't everything else all messed up?" Ned asked. "It just doesn't make any sense unless—he was here when I came back for my wallet, stopped his search, and shoved the stuff into the drawer."

"But why go to all that trouble?" Burt commented. "It seems to me that regardless of his habits, a stranger who was caught in this room by you or any of the hotel staff wouldn't have much of a defense."

"True—but suppose he *was* one of the hotel staff?" Ned proposed, letting the full weight of his deduction sink in.

"Okay, Nancy Drew," Dave said with a smirk, "who's your suspect?"

11

Undeserved Accusation

"The night clerk, of course!" Ned declared, proud of his deduction.

"The night clerk?" Burt repeated, admitting his bewilderment. "I don't understand. Why him?"

"Because when I realized I couldn't get into the room last night, I went back to the lobby and he wasn't around," Ned said.

"But that doesn't mean he was in our room," Dave pointed out.

"True, but then what about Nancy's message—the one he read over the phone? Where is it? We already agreed that it didn't sound like something she would write."

"Are you suggesting that the clerk made it up?" Burt asked, causing Ned to set his jaw firmly.

"Yes, I think so."

"And he sent us to the Lido even though he probably knew the girls weren't there," Dave put in. "Then he contacted a friend and asked him to blow up our boat!"

"Well, in that case, all we have to do is wait for him to come on duty," Dave said. "We'll take him by force, if necessary."

"Oh, sure," Burt replied, "right in the middle of the hotel lobby."

Ned noted the hour, saying that it was still early and they had plenty of time left to plan their strategy. Meanwhile, they had no other clues to where their friends were.

"All I know is, if I'm right about the clerk," Ned said, "he's probably hoping we'll book a flight home very soon. Actually, that might not be a bad idea."

"To go home and leave the girls stranded?" Dave said, incredulous.

"No, no, no. We'll just pretend we're leaving," Ned assured him.

"But how can you make believe you're leaving and not really leave?"

"By checking out of here and going to another hotel."

"I don't think it's that simple," Burt said, "because in order to make our departure look realistic, we'd have to take the hotel boat to the airport, then sneak back."

"Are you sure you want to go through all that?" Dave asked. "I mean, wouldn't it be just as easy to take our bags and walk out the door?"

"Hardly," his friends chorused.

"We can't take the chance. One of the other staff members might mention it to the night clerk," Ned pointed out, "and then we'd really be sunk."

So it was jointly decided that they would switch hotels.

"I wonder if we can find out where the clerk lives," Burt said.

"Probably not without drawing suspicion on ourselves," Ned replied.

"I don't even know his name," Dave commented. "Do either of you?"

Both boys shook their heads. "I'm sure we

can find out, though," Ned said, opening his suitcase to repack it.

Burt, meanwhile, telephoned the desk to announce their departure for the airport, prompting Dave to hunt through his guidebook for the name of another hotel.

"How about the Danielli?" he suggested.

"How about setting up a tent in the square?" Burt answered with one eyebrow raised.

"In other words, the Danielli's out," Dave said. He leafed through a few pages. "Now, here's something. The Pensione Seguso. 'Its furniture is elegantly old-fashioned and Venetian. The sitting room and dining rooms have antique, embroidered red-silk wall coverings.'"

"Well, I wouldn't consider any place that didn't have red-silk wall coverings," Burt crooned in a high-pitched voice.

"My point is, we could probably stay there without being discovered by the night clerk."

"You're right," Burt answered. "Is there a phone number for the pensione?"

Dave nodded as he dialed, and inquired about reservations. "We'll need a large room for three," he said into the receiver, then hung up. "You know, something just occurred to me.

What if the girls come back to the Gritti after we leave? We should tell them where they can find us."

"And risk having somebody open the letter?" Ned asked. "Uh-uh. We'll call them later."

"Okay, whatever you say," Dave replied, allowing the discussion to end as they got ready to leave the hotel. By the time they checked out and started for the airport as part of their ploy, it was well into the afternoon.

Nancy, Bess, and George had determined the steps they would take should their abductors return. Hoping it would be soon, they waited in the unbroken silence of their prison.

Then, several hours later, they heard the familiar clatter of shoes on the cold marble floor outside.

"Get ready," Nancy whispered to her friends.

George immediately felt her muscles tighten while Bess, quivering slightly, tried to quell her nervousness. The footsteps halted just outside the door, and someone began to push the handle, at the same time muttering in Italian. Nancy laid her hand on Bess's signaling her to remain quiet.

"Che cosa c'é che non funziona con questa porta? What's the matter with this door?" he said as the handle jiggled from side to side, convincing the young detective that it was not one of their captors. If it were, he would know there was a lug in the lock.

"It's stuck!" she called out.

"Chi c'é lí? Who's there?" the man replied, letting the knob go and causing Nancy to strain for the little Italian she knew.

"Siamo in tre. Bloccatio. Per favore aiuteteci," she said haltingly. "Three of us. Locked up. Please help."

"Where'd he go?" Bess asked as the man left in silence.

"I hope he went to get help," George answered, but to the girls' chagrin, it seemed to take forever before the stranger returned.

His voice, now low and indistinct, rose only once as someone else, probably a locksmith or a maintenance person, tried to remove the lug. After several attempts, all of them unsuccessful, he began to drill around it.

"I don't believe it," Bess said. "We're really going to get out of here."

But her optimism faded quickly as the work

on the door came to an unexpected end and the men departed.

"What's the matter? Why did they stop?" George asked, no less agitated than her two companions.

"I don't know, but I hope they come back before our captors do," Nancy said.

"Oh, Nancy, you're right," Bess replied. "What'll we do—"

"Look, let's not get ourselves upset before it happens," George interrupted, trying to relax.

But it was not until the work on the lock started again that the trio felt another glimmer of hope, and it was not until the door stood open that they believed they were free.

"*Grazie, grazie*," the girls said over and over to their rescuers, one of whom proved to be a priest.

He smiled through his owl-eyed glasses, nodding as he stepped past Nancy to look into the room. Upon sight of the rope and the gags, he gasped in horror, pointing them out to the other man in workclothes who stood behind him. Nancy showed them the deep, red impressions that circled her wrists, then indicated Bess's and George's, too.

Exclamations of horror sputtered from the priest as he took Nancy's hand and led her forward. Bess and George followed, leaving the workman behind to pick up his tools and the evidence of the girls' imprisonment. Soon they found themselves in an office at one end of the basilica, where the priest made a phone call to police headquarters.

"Here we go again," Bess murmured hopelessly, while Nancy drew the priest's attention to Antonio's card, which she had removed from her pocket. She motioned to the telephone.

"*Prego*. Go right ahead," he said, nodding.

It was nearly half an hour later when Antonio arrived on the heels of two policemen, one of whom was Captain Donatone. As quickly as she could, Nancy explained what had happened to her and her friends, and Bess described how the hotel clerk had lured her into the trap.

Antonio translated the story into Italian, drawing deep, confused frowns from his listeners.

"He says it's impossible," the young interpreter told the girls. "The priest says it is unthinkable that anyone would use the basilica as a prison."

"It may be unthinkable," George said, "but it

happened. Just look at our arms and legs."

"He does not say you are lying. Only that he cannot imagine such a thing."

"Maybe our abductors were dressed like priests," Bess offered.

There were nods of consideration followed by a loud, unconvinced sigh from Captain Donatone. He said something to the girls' interpreter that Antonio hesitated to repeat.

"What is it, Antonio?" Nancy asked.

"He says—you like this detective business too much. Maybe you like to play tricks on the police."

"What?" George replied, indignantly. "That's crazy!"

"Look, all we have to do is show him the door, the lock, and the lug," Nancy said quietly. "Besides, the priest is a witness."

But when Antonio conveyed all of this to the men, the priest suggested fetching the workman. He appeared shortly and after several minutes of conversation between himself and the police, most of which the girls did not understand, Antonio cleared his throat.

"Well?" Bess asked, hoping they had finally been vindicated.

"Well," Antonio said, "according to this man

the lug could have been put into the door from either side."

"That's preposterous!" George exclaimed.

"Calm down," Nancy told her, turning to Antonio again. "You believe us, don't you?"

"Of course."

"Then why don't the police?"

"It's not a matter of what they believe or don't believe, Miss Drew. They just think you are—how you say—meddlesome."

Nancy lowered her eyes for a second, replying in her steadiest voice, "I'd like to make an official report at headquarters anyway."

"That is your privilege," Antonio said as the girl's lips trembled, not so much from fear as determination to prove herself.

12

New Developments

The police offered to take Nancy and her friends to headquarters at once.

"I just hope they don't try to keep us there," Bess confided to her cousin as they walked toward the Rialto with Antonio.

"How could they?" George replied.

"I don't know. But I'm sure they'd figure out a way if they wanted to."

"Bess," Nancy interrupted, "do you think that you would be willing to interview the night clerk for us?"

"The night clerk—me? And wind up in another closet? Uh-uh. No thanks."

Even George looked askance at the idea.

"What makes you think he'll show up for work—especially when he finds out we escaped?" she asked.

"Well, it's only a hunch, mind you," Nancy said, "but according to my watch, he ought to be going on duty soon, in which case there'd be very little time for anyone to have reported our escape."

By now, the group had reached the familiar iron door of the police station, and the girls wasted no more conversation on the current topic. Instead, with Antonio's help, they gave a report of what had happened to them, supplying as many details as they could, including a description of the night clerk.

"I hope you realize you are making a very serious charge against this man," Antonio translated on behalf of the captain. "Perhaps you should think about it again. After all, it's possible he was simply trying to get to know you, miss, and became an innocent victim of circumstances?"

Bess shook her head resolutely. "No, Captain," she said, "*I* was the victim of circumstances."

"If you say so—but you have yet to tell me

why anyone would want to hold all of you prisoners."

That was Nancy's opportunity to reveal the conversation she had overheard in which the name Dandolo was mentioned, but she didn't say anything, honoring her promise to the *duchessa.* No one knew about Filippo's disappearance, and Nancy vowed she would not let the information slip out now.

"*Molto bene.* Very well then," Captain Donatone said, filling in the silence. "We will look into the matter further, but I cannot promise what we can do about it. I suggest, however, that you return to the States."

"We will consider it," Nancy answered politely, then asked about her Emerson friends.

Hearing they had been released the previous day, the young detectives were both elated and eager to see them.

"Can you imagine how worried they must be about us?" Bess said as they hurried back to the Gritti Palace Hotel accompanied by Antonio. "Oh, we'll have to go out for a big reunion dinner tonight! I'm absolutely famished!"

George tossed her gaze to a sign that said DO FORNI. "Then that's the restaurant for you," she announced. "Two ovens for a double-sized stomach!"

"Very funny, George," her cousin replied. Despite the grimace on her face, however, she felt a modicum of delight at being the butt of George's teasing again, which she had sorely missed during the past twenty-four hours. "You don't still want me to talk to the night clerk, do you, Nancy?" she inquired.

"It all depends. Let's see if he's around first," the girl detective said. "Actually, I'm hoping we can get to our room before he turns up—*if* he turns up." She gave a sidelong glance to George that did not pass unnoticed by Antonio.

"Perhaps it is not wise for you to stay at the Gritti," Antonio suggested.

"But it's so beautiful," Bess commented. "Oh no, we wouldn't want to stay anywhere else in Venice."

The young man smiled, spiraling his gaze toward the sky that now flushed pink in the setting sun. "Well, then, you had better run if you want to catch the view on the canal," he said. "It should be spectacular."

"'Bye, Antonio," the girls said in unison.

"We'll be sure to call if we need you," Nancy added cheerfully.

When they reached the Gritti, however, the girls' spirits sank considerably. Their friends from Emerson College had not only checked out of the hotel. They had left for home!

"I just don't believe this is happening to me," Bess groaned.

"To you?" George asked. "What about the rest of us?"

"Well, you know what I mean," Bess said, collapsing on her bed to stare at the ceiling. "First, our beautiful vacation turns into a nightmare and then Dave takes off."

"He wasn't alone, either," Nancy put in. "It just doesn't make sense. It's so unlike Ned."

"And Burt," George added, sitting in the chair by the window. "By the way, did anybody notice the night clerk lurking around?"

"No," Nancy said in a faraway voice, now feeling an uncontrollable desire to sleep.

Perhaps it was due to the stress of recent harrowing events and the fact that since the girls' arrival in Venice, they had spent little time relaxing. Whatever the reason, Nancy sank deeply into her pillow; and it wasn't until the phone rang some forty minutes later that she and the other girls awoke.

"Hello," she said, stifling a yawn as she listened to the voice at the other end. "Ned! Where are you?"

"Are they all still in Italy?" Bess asked eagerly.

Nancy motioned her to be quiet, and when she finished speaking on the phone, she said, "The boys are here, but Ned wouldn't tell me where they're staying. We'll meet them later under the belltower in the square."

"Next to the basilica?" George asked warily.

"You're sure you were talking to Ned and not somebody who sounded like him?" Bess put in quickly. "I'd hate to walk into another trap."

"If you're really worried about it," Nancy said softly, "I can see the fellows alone."

That was more than enough to spur Bess to her feet. "I wouldn't think of it. George, please hand me my cosmetic bag," she said and flew into the bathroom, poking her head out of the door for a second. "How would Dave feel if I didn't show up?"

"Beats me," George said, doing all she could to refrain from giggling at her cousin's newfound energy.

When Bess finally reappeared again, her hair was swept back in a crown of waves, but instead of asking for the girls' opinion as she usually did, she leaped to the closet.

"Guess it's my turn," George went on. "What are you wearing tonight, Bess?"

"Oh, something exotic. My silk dress perhaps," she said, referring to a cream-colored outfit that complemented her fair skin. "Of course, I was hoping to have a tan by now, but . . ."

Her words faded as she rumbled through her shoes, while Nancy made her own selection of clothes, a pretty ruffled skirt with a blouse to match and low-heeled sandals. Those, she concluded, were not only comfortable for walking but perfect for chasing any would-be assailant!

"Speaking of kidnappers—" Nancy said offhandedly.

"Oh, do we have to?" Bess put in, as she buttoned a cuff.

"It is a dreary subject," Nancy agreed, "but unfortunately it's also a reality for us. I'm sure the *duchessa* is wondering why she hasn't heard from us."

"And I'm wondering if she's been contacted again," George said. "Do you suppose we should also try seeing *her* later?"

"That's a thought," Nancy said. She picked up the phone, ready to dial the woman's private number but changed her mind. "We can call from the restaurant."

"Whew!" Bess grinned. "For a minute there, I expected you to cancel out on dinner."

Nancy grinned back. "Come on, everybody. Let's go."

When they reached the downstairs lobby, they glanced at the registration desk looking for the night clerk but he wasn't there, and Nancy inquired about him.

"Erminio Scarpa is on vacation, *signorina*," his replacement informed her. "Perhaps I can help you."

The young detective hesitated, then continued.

"Could you, by any chance, give me his home address?" Nancy asked, causing the man's face to become animated.

"As a rule, we do not—" he started to say.

"The police are looking for him," Nancy interrupted boldly.

"He tried to kidnap us," Bess blurted.

"What?" their listener answered, shaking his head in puzzlement. "That's the craziest thing I ever heard. Not only that, it's quite impossible, too. As I said, Mr. Scarpa is on vacation."

"Well, perhaps we aren't talking about the same person," Nancy said. "The man we have in mind has thick black hair that sits like a cap over his ears. He's about your height—"

"I tell you he hasn't been here," the clerk insisted, admitting that the description fit Mr. Scarpa. "Perhaps you have him mixed up with someone else."

"May we have his address, please?" George cut in.

"I'm sorry. It's against our policy. Now if you will excuse me."

The man turned on his heel, leaving the girls utterly stunned by his lack of sympathy.

"He's covering up, that's all," Bess told her friends as they headed for the piazza. "We'll just have to track Scarpa down on our own."

"That's the old spirit," George said. "Got any brilliant ideas how to do it?"

"We can start with the telephone directory," Nancy replied, "and if that fails, we'll speak to our hotel manager in the morning."

Soon the trio arrived at the belltower. The boys were there already, and Ned and his two friends hugged the girls joyfully.

"Are you ready to eat?" Burt asked. "We're starved."

"So are we," the girls replied in unison and Nancy mentioned Do Forni.

"It's supposed to have wonderful risotto," she said gleefully.

"Then let's go!" Ned exclaimed, taking her arm.

Once they were there, however, they spent less time on the meal and more on news of the past twenty-four hours. When the boys heard what had happened to their friends, they were shocked and angry.

"We tried to find you at the Lido," Ned said. "The night clerk told us that's where you went."

"That figures!" Bess groaned.

"He sent us on a wild-goose chase," Ned said, "and then told one of his buddies to sink our boat."

"There was this creep hanging from a rope," Burt muttered. "Too bad he didn't fall into the drink—"

"But we found a clue!" Dave cut in. "Ned, show Nancy the cap."

The girl looked it over carefully. "Someday

I'll find out whom this belongs to," she vowed. "But now tell us why you were thinking of flying home? Did you really believe we had left Venice?"

"Of course not," Ned said. "As a matter of fact, we—" He stopped speaking instantly as three pretty girls emerged from the restaurant doorway.

Burt and Dave had seen them too, but pretended not to, downing large helpings of the creamy rice dish in front of them. "You were right, Nancy. This risotto is spectacular," Burt said, steering George's gaze away from the threesome they had met at the Hotel Excelsior.

But upon seeing the boys, the girls waved and came forward. "Don't forget," Christine said to Dave, "we'll be here until Saturday."

As she spoke, Bess smiled pleasantly. "That's nice," she said. "We're leaving tomorrow."

"We are?" Dave coughed, gulping on his glass of water.

"Yes, if you make a date with her!" Bess giggled under her breath.

13

An Inescapable Snare

As the blush of embarrassment faded from Dave's face, Christine and the Austrian girls strode to the far end of the restaurant, leaving Ned and the other boys to explain how they had met.

"It all started with a mistaken identity," Ned said, telling about the titian-haired girl who closely resembled Nancy.

"Of course, we soon discovered she wasn't you," Burt piped up, "and we took up the hunt all over again."

"Oh, we knew you wouldn't abandon us," George said, smiling.

"And now that we're all together, we can

really help the *duchessa*!" Nancy exclaimed.

"A real *duchessa*?" Burt asked.

"Mm-hmm. She lives on San Gregorio opposite the Gritti," Bess offered, "and she wants us to find—"

The sting of her cousin's eyes caused her to stop mid-sentence. "Don't talk too loudly," George said, so Nancy could continue.

"Maybe we ought to let the *duchessa* tell you the story herself. I did promise we wouldn't discuss it with anyone."

"Including me?" Ned chuckled.

"I'm afraid so," his friend said. "But you'll hear all the details very soon." She excused herself momentarily, fishing a *gettone*, or token, out of her purse to use in the public telephone that stood near the door. "I'll only be a minute. Order me a *mascarpone* for dessert!"

"Now look who's being extravagant!" Bess laughed. "Make that *due*—two!"

When Nancy rejoined the group, she seemed less jovial; and the elegant dish in front of her registered only mild satisfaction on her face.

"Is something wrong?" Ned asked immediately.

"I'm not sure," she said. "I started to tell the

duchessa that we wanted to bring you and Burt and Dave over to meet her and she cut me off before I could finish. She said she had no need to talk to me again."

"What?" Bess replied in astonishment.

"Maybe she just isn't up to having visitors," George remarked.

"I don't think that's it," Nancy said. "She sounded perfectly fine, not at all tired, but something was definitely wrong. I wish I knew what it was."

She took one spoonful of dessert, then let the utensil fall on the dish, a spark of sudden awareness in her eyes.

"She said, 'Do not come now. I do not need only you,'" Nancy repeated. "The way she spoke sounded so awkward."

"Maybe she was trying to tell you just the opposite of what she meant," George said.

"Exactly," Nancy replied, as Ned asked the waiter for the bill.

"How do we get to San Gregorio?" the boy said shortly.

"By *vaporetto*, *motoscafo*, or—how about taking a *traghetto*?" Bess grinned.

"Since when did you learn so much Italian?"

George asked her cousin teasingly, "and what on earth is a *traghetto*?"

"It's a short ride in a gondola from one side of the canal to the other. Is there anything else you'd like to know?" Bess continued, laughing lightly as the group left the restaurant.

"Not just now, thank you," her cousin said, and hurried ahead with Burt, who was aiming for a fleet of gondolas parked behind the restaurant.

"I gather we're going to take a *traghetto*," Bess called out breathlessly. She stopped to adjust the strap on her shoe, but Dave grabbed her hand before she could do so.

"Come, Miss Italy. The boat's going to leave without us!" he exclaimed.

"Oh, it is not," she said. Nevertheless, she picked up her pace, soon finding herself and her friends in one of several gondolas, all of them filled with eager tourists whose voices barely tittered under the booming shouts of the gondoliers.

"Isn't this fun?" Bess said. She leaned against her seat to watch the lead boat with its jaunty pilot.

He had begun to serenade his passengers,

singing a familiar tune to the black silky sky that loomed fuller as they glided down the narrow canal.

"I have a feeling we should have gone to the gondola station on the square," Nancy murmured impatiently.

"We'll make it," Ned assured her, touching her hand. Burt, however, made a different observation.

"I'd say we're in for a traffic jam," he said, as the oars stopped turning and the gondolas came to a halt just at the edge of the Grand Canal.

Shouts relayed from one gondolier to another, and Ned turned to theirs, asking what the trouble was, but the man did not hear him as he yelled out to no one in particular. Then, as if by magic, the gondolas began to move again. Just before they slid under a low bridge, Nancy detected a pair of green fiery eyes staring down at her from a first-floor window of a building on the canal.

"Oh, Ned, look," she said. "Have you ever seen such a big black cat?"

"I hope it's not an omen for the future," the boy said, laughing, but his comment slipped past Nancy as she noticed a man's profile in the same window.

His hair, thick and black, lay caplike over his ear!

"That's the night clerk from the hotel!" she exclaimed, drawing the others' attention to the window. But it was empty now and the gondola had swept away too quickly, leaving in its wake only a vague impression of the window's location.

"At least, we know he's still in Venice," Nancy said. "I intend to come back here tomorrow and check out that building."

As she spoke, the gondolas, still hugging together, turned up the canal, and George asked if anyone had bothered to tell the gondolier where they wanted to be taken.

"I didn't," Burt said.

"Neither did I," Ned chimed in. "I thought you did."

"Don't look at me," Dave said, causing Nancy to motion to the oarsman.

"We—want—to—go—over—there," she said. "*Prego.*"

But the man shook his head, and she wasn't

sure if that meant no or he didn't understand.

"*Prego*," she began again, pointing toward the building in the near distance where a lamp shone in the *duchessa*'s apartment.

Still the man didn't respond, and the lead gondolier began to sing, drawing the whole flotilla in line with each other and letting Nancy's words fade under the applause.

"You know what?" Bess whispered to the young detective.

"What?" she said, already suspecting the answer.

"I think we're part of a tour group."

George groaned disgustedly. "This could take hours!"

"And by then who knows what may have happened to the *duchessa*?" Nancy said anxiously. "Oh, Ned, this is terrible. We have to do something."

The only idea that occurred to him had worked once before; but the question was, would it work now?

"Ned, please!" Nancy persisted as she watched the gondolier dip and turn the oars again.

It was almost unbearable to feel the craft surging forward, away from the troubled woman's home; and the painful look in Nancy's eyes was all it took to send the boy into action.

14

Strange Behavior

Ned leaped to his feet, causing the gondola to tilt sideways while he removed his jacket.

"What are you doing, Ned?" Nancy cried while their gondolier poured out a warning.

"Sit down, sit down," he shouted in Italian.

"Ned, please," Nancy added.

"But you—" her friend started to say, prompting the girl to repeat her plea.

"I didn't mean for you to swim to our destination," she said, relieved when he was seated once again. "As for the *duchessa* . . . well, I'll just say a prayer for her that she's all right."

By now they had drifted further up the Grand Canal, passing graceful palaces built from the twelfth century to the present, their unlit facades a sad reminder of the powerful men and women and great artists who no longer lived there.

"I wouldn't mind having my own personal palazzo," Dave remarked.

"Then, how about that one?" Nancy asked pointing to a building with festive gold-trimmed poles in front of it. But when she saw that it was a museum, she retracted her suggestion. "I'm afraid the Guggenheim isn't for sale." She laughed.

"I wonder if they still keep a lion in the garden," Ned put in.

"A what?" Nancy asked.

"A lion. The Guggenheim was originally called the Palazzo Venier Dei Leoni because, according to tradition, the Veniers had a pet lion."

"Now I've heard everything," George commented, watching a preoccupied look slowly blossom in Nancy's face.

The young detective had tried hard not to think about her awkward conversation with the *duchessa*, but it continued to haunt her. And if it weren't for George's sudden canting interruption, Nancy would not have hesitated to voice her thoughts aloud.

"'And there afloat on the placid sea . . . lay a great city,'" George said, recalling a passage from a book she had once read. "'Gondolas were gliding swiftly hither and thither. Everywhere there was a hush.'"

"Bravo. Thank you," Bess cheered. "That was beautiful."

"Well, don't thank me. Thank Mark Twain." George dimpled her cheeks in a smile. "He came to Venice sometime in the 1860s and wrote about it in *Innocents Abroad.*"

"You know," Nancy said, joining in the conversation, "according to tradition, the gondola evolved when the first people who lived on the lagoon got caught in high tide and had to paddle with their hands!"

I hope we won't have to do that!" Bess exclaimed.

"Don't worry, silly," George chided her. "This gondola is perfectly balanced, isn't it, Nancy?"

"Yes, they're all built to very specific dimensions. Not only that, but the boat is made up of some two hundred and eighty pieces of wood. Altogether, they weigh over a thousand pounds!"

"In other words, banish your fears, Bess." Burt chortled. "Besides, see that iron piece on the prow? On top of those six teeth is the Doge's hat. He'll watch over you."

"I'd rather Dave," the girl replied, mockingly defiant, as she coaxed his arm around her.

When the tour finally ended, the young people walked to the Gritti and Nancy called the Dandolo residence again. This time there was no answer.

"She must have gone out," Nancy said, worried.

"Or to bed," George pointed out. "It is late, you know."

The young people managed to find a gondolier to take them across the canal. When they arrived at the *duchessa*'s apartment, however, the door was securely locked and no one answered their insistent rings.

"She could be out. She could be sleeping, or she could be in trouble," Nancy concluded in distress.

"Personally, I think that you're letting your

imagination run away with you," Bess said. "I mean even though the phone message was a bit strange, it wasn't a desperate cry for help either."

"I agree," George said. "Anyway, it seems to me you ought to wait until morning and try to contact her again."

Nancy did not answer, but hesitantly, she examined the lock.

"You can't just break into someone's apartment," Ned said, pulling her away.

"Okay. You're right. Let's go back to the Gritti," the girl sighed. "I just hope the *duchessa* will be able to tell me tomorrow what she was trying to say tonight."

"How about coming to our *pensione* for breakfast?" Ned suggested when they reached the other side of the canal. "It isn't the Gritti, but it's very comfortable and the food is quite good."

"Sounds great!" Bess said, accepting the invitation for everyone. "'Bye!"

The girls awoke early, and Nancy made a notation to leave a message for her father should he call from Rome while she was out.

"Dad's due in tonight," she told her friends,

"and I'm sure he'll phone the minute he arrives."

As she spoke, she picked up the receiver to dial the Dandolo residence. There were four long rings before anyone answered, then came a hello that temporarily startled the girl.

"Andreoli?" she said, recognizing the deep-chested voice.

"*Si.*"

"This is Nancy Drew. Is the *duchessa* there?"

"*No. No . . . arrivederci.*"

"Wait . . . Andreoli," Nancy said, but the man had already clicked off the line. "I have to go over there right away," she announced immediately.

"What about breakfast?" Bess asked. "Can't you—"

"You go ahead without me," Nancy replied. "I'll join you as soon as I can."

"I'm coming with you," George decided. "Bess, how about you going to meet the boys?"

"Sure," Bess said. "But, are you sure you two will be all right?"

"Don't worry," Nancy said. "We'll be fine."

Since Ned hadn't called yet, Nancy gave Bess

the *pensione's* address and the trio parted company. Nancy and George said nothing, however, until they reached their destination. Then they knocked fiercely on the downstairs door.

"Hello! Anybody there?" Nancy called out. To her relief, it finally opened, revealing Andreoli, the gondolier. His face was very pale, almost sickly, and there was no smile of greeting.

"The *duchessa*, where is she?" Nancy asked.

"Not here," the man replied crisply before lapsing into Italian and making the girls' eyebrows furrow quizzically.

The only word they understood was Murano, the largest island in the Venetian lagoon and the site of several glass-making factories, among them Artistico Vetro! Had the *duchessa* gone to visit Filippo's father?

She must have, Nancy decided, but why so suddenly?

Unable to communicate her questions to Andreoli, she sensed an unexplained nervousness about him, possibly the result of his concern for the woman's whereabouts. Whatever the reason, though, he pushed the door forward, indicating he had no more to say. But Nancy poised her hand against it.

"May we go upstairs?" she asked on impulse. How do I say it in Italian? "Andreoli, *di sopra*."

The gondolier hesitated, holding the door in place, then pulled it back slowly with great reluctance. He led the way up the wooden flight and stopped a few steps before the landing as if he had changed his mind. The girls, however, had already glimpsed the unexpected scene beyond the half-open door at the top. The drawers of the desk stood open, their contents strewn on the floor!

"What happened?" Nancy asked, leaping past the gondolier.

He hurried after her and shook his head, spilling out an answer, which trailed after her as she darted from room to room to see if anything else was out of order. Satisfied that nothing was, she figured the intruder had found what he was looking for and departed quickly.

Knowing just how secretive the *duchessa* had been about her nephew's disappearance, Nancy now understood Andreoli's reluctance to show her the living room.

He's probably afraid I'll report the intrusion to the police, the girl decided, trying to assure the gondolier otherwise. But discussion with him proved hopeless, prompting her and

George to say good-bye quickly. They had not asked their boatman to wait for them so they headed for the landing-stage up the street.

Unlike previous sojourns on the *vaporetto*, there were fewer passengers onboard this time. Their eyes were attracted to the dappling of sunlight on the water while Nancy's were only vaguely fixed. What had the intruder been searching for? she wondered, then the most obvious answer struck. A copy of the glass formula!

Of course! Why didn't I think of that right away? Nancy thought as she and George hurried to the Pensione Seguso.

When they finally arrived, Ned asked them what had taken so long. "We were beginning to get worried," he said.

Nancy gulped in a deep breath and took the seat opposite him. "I'm sorry . . . really," she replied as a waiter quickly introduced the menu to her. Food, however, was the last thing on her mind; she ordered only one poached egg.

"Is that all you want?" George asked, offering her the basket of rolls.

"I'm not very hungry this morning," Nancy

said, and proceeded to tell about her visit with Andreoli. "It's too bad Antonio wasn't with us."

"Who's Antonio?" Burt inquired, drawing a quick reminder from George about the student who had accompanied the girls on their visits to police headquarters.

"Oh . . . sorry for the interruption, Nancy. Please go on," the boy said. When she finished speaking, he and his Emerson friends exchanged glances.

"Do we foresee an unexpected trip to Murano?" Ned asked.

"Yes, most definitely," Nancy answered. "It occurred to me that the *duchessa* might have followed the intruder there, but somehow I just can't imagine it. She's not exactly feeble, yet I would have thought Andreoli would have taken her."

"Do you think she was kidnapped, too?" Bess asked.

"Possibly."

"Well, I suppose that we'll be able to find a boat to take us to Murano right now, if you like," Ned said, but Nancy's mind was on the night clerk whom she had seen in the window the previous evening.

"I have to make one small investigation first," she remarked with a glance at her watch. "I'm going to visit Scarpa's apartment. Do you all want to wait for me here or shall I meet you somewhere?"

"Why don't we go with you?" Ned suggested.

"A whole group might be too conspicuous. It's better if I go alone. I won't be long," Nancy said, pausing. "How about meeting at one o'clock under the clock tower? You could line up a boat for Murano in the meantime."

Before anyone could object, the girl stood up, kissed Ned lightly on the cheek, and dashed out of the dining room.

Using the restaurant Do Forni as her starting point, she wandered along the street looking at the names above the residents' doorbells. To her chagrin, Scarpa was not among them.

"I'll never find the building this way," she muttered to herself and went back to the gondolas stationed behind the restaurant.

Before stepping into one of them, she instructed the gondolier to take her through the narrow canal only. "Grand Canal—no," she added firmly.

"*Si, signorina*. No Grand Canal."

Somehow, perhaps because of the lazy feeling created by the warmth of the day, the ride seemed particularly long to Nancy. They floated past a row of peeling brick buildings that melted into one another without distinction. But as the gondolier dug his oar under the bridge, two tigerish eyes sprang into view behind the elusive half-open window; and Nancy felt her blood race.

15

Sisterly Protection

At the sight of the familiar black cat in the window, Nancy gasped, holding her breath for a second and wondering if its master was there too. She signaled the gondolier to stop at a small landing-stage up ahead where she stepped off and hurried down the short alleyway next to the building.

Suddenly, from an iron balcony neatly lined with small pots of red geraniums, the young detective heard a distinct meow as two of the pots suddenly fell against the grating and the feline flew to the ground in a single leap, landing on all fours. Nancy froze, glancing upward just in time to see the window click shut.

Someone is up there, she decided and quickly sidestepped the animal.

As she suspected, there was no name on the front door but to her surprise it was open. She entered cautiously, not seeing the figure above her who spoke shortly.

"Who are you?" the woman asked.

Nancy felt a disquieting tremor pass through her body as she gazed at the crippled form above her.

"I am a guest at the Gritti Palace Hotel," she replied, not wishing to reveal her name, "and I am looking for a Mr. Erminio Scarpa. I thought he lived here."

"Come up, please," the woman replied. She dragged her legs away from the door, relying on two canes for support.

"I hope I'm not disturbing you," Nancy commented, climbing the wooden stairs.

"Not at all," her listener said and indicated a comfortable chair in the living room, which the girl took. "It is my pleasure."

Nancy noticed the simple yet tasteful furnishings in the apartment, along with a small collection of photographs on a corner table. One in particular drew her attention, but she waited for the woman to speak before inquiring about it.

The woman politely introduced herself as Lucia, and then came abruptly to the point.

"Why are you looking for my brother?" she asked and laid her canes down by her chair, causing Nancy to reconsider her approach.

Did she dare reveal all her suspicions to the man's sister? It stood to reason she would be protective of him, and would she not learn more from Nancy than the young detective wanted her to know? Nevertheless, Nancy proceeded with her questioning.

"I am a detective—"

"You?" the woman said in surprise. "But you are so young."

Nancy smiled. "I'm just an amateur detective," she explained, adding that she had been asked to investigate a matter that had recently occurred at the Gritti Palace Hotel.

"How recently?" her listener inquired.

"Within the past few days."

"Well, I doubt that Erminio could be of much help to you. He's on vacation, you know."

"Have you not seen him then?"

"No—not since last week."

"And you have been in this apartment all this time?" Nancy replied.

The woman seemed hesitant to answer. "No,

but what does that have to do with my brother?" she asked.

Although Nancy had carefully avoided making accusations against the man, it was evident that Lucia was uneasy, as if she also had some hidden anxiety about him.

"I thought I saw him last evening," Nancy said finally.

"Impossible," the woman snapped back. "Besides, what do you want with him?"

"I'm afraid I will have to talk to him directly."

As she talked, her eyes darted to a photograph on the table. In it were four people, including Lucia and Erminio. The third person was a pretty, dark-haired woman who bore a slight resemblance to them and next to her was a handsome young man. It was his face that had caught Nancy's attention.

"Is this a family picture by any chance?" the girl inquired, rising from her seat to look at it more closely.

"Yes and no," Lucia said. "That is my younger sister. She is presently in Switzerland, visiting friends."

"And the young man—is he a younger brother?" Nancy continued.

In the short silence that ensued, she found herself staring at the features of the young man in the photo. Although the gap in their ages was considerable, the comely expression was the same. Yes, indeed, he looked very much like the *duchessa* herself!

"No," Lucia said faintly, "he was a friend of my sister's." She did not volunteer any other information about him. "I am sorry my brother is not here to talk to you, but I will tell him you came."

"When do you expect to see him again?" Nancy asked.

"Oh, not for some time yet."

Not surprised by the answer, the young detective thanked the woman for her help and left. In a strange way, her visit had proved successful. She secreted her discoveries in the back of her mind, hopeful she would soon figure out the Scarpa connection with the Dandolo family.

Noting the time as she walked toward the piazza, Nancy quickened her steps. It was well past one o'clock, and she knew that her friends would probably be worried. As she turned the corner, she heard footfalls running in her direction from behind, then an arm grabbed hers.

"Ned! Where'd you come from?" Nancy said in amazement.

"Some detective you are," he teased. "Didn't even know I followed you from the *pensione*, did you?"

"Nope."

"Well, I thought you might have needed some unexpected assistance."

"That's really nice of you," the young detective said, admitting some slight trepidation about meeting Scarpa face to face. "As it turned out, though, I met his sister instead."

"Hm-mm," Ned replied. "You'll have to tell us all about it on the way to Murano."

"We have a boat, then?" Nancy asked.

"As you requested, *signorina*," the boy said, taking her hand and running across the square.

Having told the others of his plan to track after Nancy, Ned had asked Burt and Dave to arrange for the outing and shifted the meeting place from the clock tower to the nearby dock.

"How does it feel to have your very own shadow?" George quipped as Nancy and Ned stepped aboard the launch.

"It feels great." Nancy smiled. She waited

until they were underway, however, before she told about her encounter with Lucia Scarpa.

"Do you suppose the guy in that photograph is Filippo Dandolo?" Bess asked eagerly. "I mean, he could be another relative of the *duchessa*'s."

"That's true," Nancy said, "but I have a strong hunch it is Filippo. Now I'm more curious than ever about all of this business. We just have to find his aunt."

By the time the group finished talking, they were halfway to Murano, having cut through the lagoon past several smaller islands toward a gate of open waters.

"Isn't it wonderful?" Bess crooned, as the boat picked up speed, sending a fine, briny spray over her.

Dave coughed lightly. "If you don't mind taking a shower in the middle of the ocean!" he exclaimed.

"Oh, you. You're so unromantic," the girl said.

The island loomed closer now, and the driver throttled the engine, letting the boat chug into shore the last few yards.

"It's not exactly a tropical paradise," Ned

whispered to Nancy, who had made a similar observation.

Even so, the immediate view was of the factory, Artistico Vetro, and that satisfied her more than enough. She ran down the paved walkway to an entrance that led into a room filled with several kilns and supply shelves. She approached a man in gloves and work apron who was firing something in one of the ovens.

"I'm looking for Signore Dandolo," Nancy said.

The man shrugged. "Not here."

"Where is he?"

"Do not know."

"What about the *duchessa*?" the young detective persisted. "Has she been here?"

"No. She never come."

As he answered, he punctuated the remark by twirling his stick of white-hot glass for the last time. Nancy, at the same time, was alerted to someone moving about in an enclosed room several yards away. The door was closed, but the small window facing the ovens revealed a woman with gray hair.

But she slipped out of sight so quickly the girl could not see her features. Still, Nancy was almost positive it was Maria Dandolo!

16

Inquiries

"Who—who was that in there?" Nancy asked the glassmaker.

"Nothing in there—storeroom," he replied in a casual tone. "No one there."

Instantly, Nancy ran to the door and tried to open it, but to her dismay, it was locked.

"*Duchessa*! It's me, Nancy Drew!" she called out, "and I brought my friends with me!"

The girl stopped, however, when she realized that there was no one behind the window, only sacks of supplies.

"She's gone!" Nancy said, concluding there must be another door to the storage room although it was not immediately visible.

For a moment, she glanced back at the

glassmaker whose concentration on his work had begun to falter. He volleyed a warning in Italian, telling the visitors to leave or else. Nancy, however, was determined to pursue her investigation.

"Is there a showroom?" she asked the man, undaunted by his blazing eyes.

"*Si*, but it is closed."

Despite the pronouncement, the young detectives hurried out of the factory and down the pavement once more, quickly discovering an adjoining building. To their delight, the entrance was open and they sped up the carpeted stairway with its steel railing glistening brightly under a magnificent handcrafted chandelier.

"Someone has to be here," Nancy said, darting into a room filled with shelves of stemware.

The lights were on and a recent order lay next to a pen on a table that Nancy focused on briefly. She was struck by the design on the paper. It was Filippo's well-known signature, the lion of Venice!

"Look, everybody!" she exclaimed, pointing to it as someone paused behind them in the doorway.

"May I help you?" the man inquired.

"I hope so," Nancy said. "Are you Signore Dandolo, by any chance?" she asked.

The man pressed his lips into a broad smile, showing an overlap of teeth that detracted from his otherwise rugged face. "No, I am not Signore Dandolo. I am Mr. Chiais, the new manager here," he said. "The *signore* has retired."

"He has?" Ned spoke up.

"Yes, now, may I show you something? Some fine glasses like these perhaps." He took a pair of exquisite goblets from a shelf and held them toward the light, revealing tiny flecks of gold leaf in the ball of the stem. "These are the most beautiful of all."

"Oh, they are," Bess commented.

But Nancy still had her thoughts on the storeroom. "Of course, you know the *duchessa*," she went on.

"Of course," the manager said.

"Well, have you seen her recently?" Nancy asked coyly, watching his eyes roam from the shelf to the table, where he had placed the two glasses.

"No, she never comes here."

"Nancy thinks she saw her, though," Bess challenged in reply.

"Oh, really. Not around here, I don't imagine," Mr. Chiais answered, as the girl fell silent under her cousin's gaze of warning.

"As a matter of fact, I did," Nancy admitted.

The manager let out a nervous laugh, saying, "I'm sure it is a case of mistaken identity. She is too old to take boat trips to Murano."

"Mr. Chiais," Nancy interposed, "how long have you been in charge here?"

"A few weeks or so. Now—are you interested in any of these glasses?" he continued, taking two more off the shelf.

"Not really," the girl replied, "but I would like to see the factory storage room."

"That is out of the question," the man said. "Only the Dandolo family is permitted inside."

"Even though Signore Dandolo is retired and the *duchessa* never comes here?" Nancy asked.

"Look, *signorina*," he went on, fiercely defensive, "I cannot—it is not within my power to show you something that is quite frankly none of your business."

Nancy stiffened, feeling Ned's consoling hand on her shoulder. "I suppose we ought to be going then," she said, much to the surprise of her friends, who deduced she was already on the verge of a new plan.

She turned on her heel, letting George march

out first. But as they stood at the edge of the stairway ready to descend, Nancy's eyes fastened on the crystal pieces in the opposite room. They included sculptures and glass etchings, all of them exquisite.

"You take the same door to leave please," Mr. Chiais called as the group stepped into the second room. "We are closing now," he noted sternly, but not before Nancy had observed Filippo's distinctive signature on several pieces.

"We'll be back," the young detective said with a courteous smile and followed her companions outside.

"Let's pretend we're leaving and go to the landing stage," she said. "Then we'll circle back and watch the factory. It should be shutting down soon, and I want to see if the *duchessa* comes out."

"Good idea," Dave said. "We can hide behind the bushes across the way."

Within a few minutes, everyone had stationed themselves accordingly. The wait, however, proved longer than they anticipated. It was almost an hour before the last workman left.

Then, suddenly, a gray-haired woman in a

fashionable suit emerged. She walked out of sight with almost imperious steps.

"Nancy, maybe that's the person you saw," George remarked under her breath. "She could pass for the *duchessa* from a distance. Only this woman's a lot younger."

Ruefully, Nancy had to admit George was right. Still, the young detectives waited for the manager to leave as well.

As soon as he locked the door behind him, Burt said, "I guess that's it for tonight. Everybody has gone home."

Nancy agreed. "Let's go, too."

"What's next on the agenda?" Ned asked.

"How about dinner?" Bess declared, suggesting the girls return to the Gritti to freshen up first. "We can meet at the belltower again."

Everyone adopted the idea instantly. But when Nancy, Bess, and George arrived in their hotel room, the phone was already ringing.

"Maybe it's your father, Nancy," George said.

The look on Nancy's face as she answered it suggested otherwise.

"Oh—*Duchessa*, I'm so glad you called!" she exclaimed. "Are you home now?"

There was a long pause, increasing the cousins' suspense and prompting them to gaze searchingly at their companion.

"What is she saying?" Bess whispered eagerly as the conversation continued.

"Oh, I see," Nancy said into the receiver. "Well—perhaps. Just a minute." She held the phone away, pondering her reply, then spoke to the woman again. "Yes, I'll be glad to come. Besides, I have a lot to report. Yes, I will. *Arrivederci*!

"The *duchessa* wants to see me," the girl went on after she hung up. "At the showroom in Murano."

"So she *is* there," George murmured, overlooking the perplexity in her friend's voice.

"Then why didn't she speak to you when you saw her?" Bess inquired.

"It was probably the other woman I saw," Nancy replied. "The *duchessa* didn't mention knowing we were there—if in fact that really was the *duchessa* who called."

"So are you going back to Murano?" George asked tensely.

"Tonight at ten."

"Not alone I hope."

"Well, she stressed that I ought to."

"Uh-uh," Bess commented. "I wouldn't do that if I were you. You could be sailing right into a big Venetian trap!"

The identical thought had occurred to Nancy, and she dived into her closet, removing a dark, ankle-length skirt from a hanger along with a high-collared silk blouse. Then she hunted for her small disguise kit that she always carried when she traveled.

Realizing what their detective friend was up to, Bess puffed her cheeks anxiously. "George and I absolutely refuse to allow you to do this," she declared. "It's too dangerous!"

"Not if she has her own personal chauffeur and judo expert!" George exclaimed, donning the souvenir gondolier's hat she had purchased earlier. "At your service, *Duchessa*!"

17

Cagey Calls

As George finished her statement with a deep bow, Nancy shook her head. "I thought of masquerading as the *duchessa*, but that could be just as dangerous as showing up as Nancy Drew," she said.

"So maybe you ought to pick a disguise somewhere in between," Bess suggested.

"Precisely," Nancy went on. "Dark hair, different style, a few lines on the face, and—"

"*Voilà!* You're thirty years older!" Her friend giggled. "Brilliant, my dear detective!"

"I don't know how brilliant it is, but I hope it helps me past the guards if there are any; and even if that phone call from the *duchessa* was on the up-and-up, I'm sure she won't mind my little charade."

"You know, I'm beginning to think you'd be safer with a football captain at your side than with me!" George exclaimed.

"We all ought to go along," Bess said. "There's greater safety in numbers."

"I don't agree," Nancy said. "I'm sure two can investigate more efficiently and secretively than six. I'll call Ned to see what he says."

The boy concurred fully with his friend's plan. "Just don't disguise yourself before we have dinner," Ned said in a teasing voice.

"Don't worry. I won't change one strand of hair until afterwards."

When the group was all together, though, Ned's bantering tone faded. "Maybe we ought to go armed with the local police force," he told Nancy.

"We can't," she said, keeping her voice barely above a whisper. "The *duchessa* would have a fit if she thought I had told you all about Filippo's kidnapping—never mind the police!"

"But what if the same thing happened to her?" Burt supported Ned.

"I still can't take the risk of telling the police

anything," Nancy said. "She made me promise."

"Okay, okay," Dave acknowledged, "but you shouldn't refuse a back-up team—"

"In case you both get stuck for some reason," Bess joined in.

"I'm hoping we won't, but if we do, I'd feel better knowing the rest of you are safe on Venetian soil and can send reinforcements, if need be."

"That's a good point," Dave admitted. "But how will we know what you've found or didn't find?"

"And how will we know you're all right?" George asked.

"There are phones everywhere at the factory," Nancy pointed out. "We'll call you the minute we arrive."

"But the switchboard probably shuts down after hours," Bess retorted.

"Then . . ." Nancy laughed, snapping her fingers. "I'll send a seagull with a message!"

Although her lighthearted response did not bring a smile to anyone's face, Ned was finally convinced that they should proceed as planned. The others would be certain to alert the police if they didn't hear from the couple by morning.

"Besides," Nancy said, "what if something turns up while we're gone that requires the attention of four skilled detectives?"

The question, however, went unanswered as they left the restaurant. Ned and Nancy made arrangements to meet at the dock from where they had taken the boat to Murano.

"See you in an hour," the boy said, as they left in separate directions.

But when Nancy and the girls reached their hotel room again, she was unprepared for the message waiting for her.

"It's from Andreoli," the girl told her friends. "He is going to call me at eight-thirty."

"Aren't you supposed to meet Ned then?" George responded.

"Yes, but it's only a five-minute walk to the square," Nancy replied. "Besides, Andreoli doesn't speak much English so I'm sure I won't be on the phone long."

She stuck her head out the window, glancing toward the empty gondola station, then drew the curtains and disappeared into the bathroom carrying the disguise kit. When she emerged a while later, the girls were duly impressed by the remarkable transformation that had occurred.

"Well?" Nancy asked, smoothing her hair. "What do you think?"

"If I didn't know better," George said, "I'd say you were a middle-aged dowager!" Bess crowed.

Nancy's usually soft reddish-blond hair was now quite brown and pressed back into an elegant knot. Her face had also been powdered to look wan and, using an eyebrow pencil, she had created lines under her eyes and across her forehead.

"Who's Ned going as? Father Time?" Bess quipped.

"I don't look that ancient, do I?" Nancy asked, chuckling. "Maybe George will lend him her gondolier's hat."

"Why not?" the girl said. "Just make sure you don't get caught, that's all. I want my hat back!"

Before Nancy had the opportunity to comment, however, Andreoli's call interrupted unexpectedly early. To Nancy's astonishment, he suddenly seemed to have acquired greater fluency in English.

"Miss Drew," he began, "I have heard from

the *duchessa.* She told me to tell you she has found her nephew. There is no more for you to do."

As the words rang in her ears, Nancy caught herself questioning the identity of the caller. The voice was familiar and at first she believed it belonged to Andreoli; but when she finally put down the receiver, having only said a brief good-bye, she gaped at her friends.

"What's the matter?" George asked, watching Nancy's pallid face turn crimson.

"That was Erminio Scarpa!" she announced.

"Huh?" Bess replied in utter amazement.

"I'm positive," Nancy said. "He called himself Andreoli, but his English was too good."

"Oh, Nancy," Bess said, her anxiety blossoming again, "please don't go to Murano!"

"I have to. Suppose the *duchessa* is being held a prisoner there?"

"In her own factory?" George asked.

Without defending the point further, the young detective took off her robe and put on the blouse and skirt she had chosen for the occasion.

"How about wearing this too?" Bess said, offering Nancy her evening shawl.

"Oh, that's perfect," the girl said. She checked her watch. "It's eight-thirty. I wonder if the message we received really was from Andreoli or Scarpa?"

"Why don't you wait five more minutes just to be sure?" Bess suggested.

"Okay."

But no other call came, and Nancy finally left her companions. When she was gone, they confessed to a mutual feeling of uneasiness. Should they abide by Nancy's request and not follow her, or ignore the young detective's instructions entirely?"

"Let's discuss it with Burt and Dave," Bess suggested. "I don't trust myself to make this sort of decision, do you?"

"No, ma'am," her cousin replied. "Besides, what if we do something against Nancy's wishes and it backfires?"

Bess breathed heavily, whistling a sigh. "We're really on the spot, aren't we?"

18

Unexpected Arrival

The two remaining couples had telephoned and decided to meet at the entrance to a park not far from dockside after Nancy and Ned were safely on their way to Murano. Bess and George, however, had lingered in their hotel room until after nine o'clock, thinking that Mr. Drew might call, and that would be their opportunity to ask his advice as well.

"Burt and Dave will be wondering where we are," George finally said. "We'd better go."

"I guess so," Bess said uneasily, following her to the elevator.

When they reached the lobby, though, they saw a porter carrying in a suitcase from the hotel float. Directly behind him was Nancy's father!

"Mr. Drew!" Bess and George cried out.

"Why, hello, girls!" he replied, looking beyond them for a sign of his daughter.

"Nancy isn't here," George whispered out of earshot of anyone else.

The secrecy in her voice carved a frown on the attorney's face, and he registered as quickly as he could, following the porter to his room. Then he hurried back to the lobby where the cousins waited for him.

"Now will you please tell me what happened?" he asked.

George explained that they were already late for their date with Burt and Dave and suggested they head for the park.

"You know, it's funny how I had to shift my plans around," Mr. Drew told the girls on the way, "only to discover Nancy is missing."

"Oh, she's not missing," Bess reassured him.

"Well, I'm glad to hear that, at least," the man said, walking briskly toward the square.

"We didn't know you were coming to Venice today," she continued.

"I didn't either," Mr. Drew replied. "My

flight was changed because of a last-minute call from my client, and I had to make a stopover in London on the way. As it is, I don't have to go to Rome until the day after tomorrow, so I thought I'd surprise Nancy by coming here first."

"Believe me, we couldn't be happier," George said.

She smiled affectionately at the man as she and Bess caught sight of the Emerson boys standing near the park wall. Upon seeing the girls and Mr. Drew, they darted forward.

"Mr. Drew!" Dave shouted loudly, causing Bess to raise a finger to her lips. George motioned everyone toward some benches away from strolling passers-by.

"Nancy told us you were going to Rome, Mr. Drew," Burt said, ferreting out the same explanation the lawyer had given the cousins.

"What's happened to Nancy? I assume Ned's with her," the man said.

"You're right," Bess replied and revealed his daughter's plan, which, in view of her past ploys to uncover secret information, did not seem too extraordinary.

"Sounds pretty clever to me," Mr. Drew remarked, "but I can't say I'm happy that she and Ned went to Murano alone."

"That's what worries us," George admitted. "As a matter of fact, Bess and I were wondering if we shouldn't take a boat out there ourselves."

As she said this, Nancy and Ned were watching the night lamps around the factory penetrate the mist that had crawled over the island.

"It's not exactly the warmest night of the year either," Nancy said, pulling her shawl closer, as their boat driver put on one final burst of speed. "Ned, please ask him to shut off his lights."

"Will do," the boy replied, and within seconds the driver cut his engine, letting the boat idle forward in the darkness.

Upon reaching the landing stage, Ned paid him the round-trip fare and asked him to wait. Then, he strode with Nancy to the factory.

To their delight, no one was on guard to scrutinize them at close range and perhaps send them back to Venice. On the other hand, there was an iron grating across the factory door that bore a large padlock.

"Well, we knew it wouldn't be easy to get

inside," Nancy murmured, moving along the building to a closed window.

Despite the chill in the air, the girl dismantled her shawl, throwing it over Ned's shoulder while he lifted her up to push the frame.

"It's locked," Nancy said when it refused to budge. "Now what?" she sighed, sliding down again.

"This way," Ned directed. He had observed a second door hidden in the shadows of a vine trellis. They walked toward it, discovering it was open! "Come on," the boy whispered and started to go in.

But Nancy quickly pulled him back, cautioning him to wait while she pressed her ear to the door. Hearing nothing, though, she pushed it back gently and took one step, then another until she was satisfied no one was behind it.

Suddenly, a light flickered in the adjoining building that housed the showroom, and Ned jumped, startling his companion.

"That must be your appointment," he said.

"I know," Nancy replied.

But she was determined to investigate the factory before making an appearance. She hurried on tiptoe toward the storage room, trying the door without success and digging into her purse for a hairpin.

"How about this?" Ned asked, producing his small penknife and pushing one of its multiple blades into the hole.

He turned it back and forth gently. For a moment he thought he heard a click, but realized it was only his imagination.

"Let me try it, Ned," Nancy said, slipping the hairpin in next, then dropping it in favor of a small, stiff postcard she found in her purse. She worked it against the bolt until it snapped! "Follow me," she whispered, pulling out a pocketsized flashlight.

The storeroom, which at first glance seemed to be no more than a small appendage to the factory, proved to be deceivingly large with metal supply shelves against the back wall and sacks of potash and lime under them. But contrary to what she had thought earlier, there was no other door besides the one they had just opened.

"I don't see the *duchessa* anywhere, do you?" Ned said, smiling into the shadows at Nancy.

"She's supposed to be waiting for me in the

showroom. Remember?" Nancy chuckled. She felt her way past a long worktable, saying nothing more until her heel caught the edge of a floorboard.

"Find something?" Ned asked.

"Could be. I'm not sure."

The young detective flashed her light along the wood, stopping on three small hinges and a thick metal bar that stretched across the opposite edge.

"It's a trapdoor! Let's try to open it," the girl urged, while Ned dropped her shawl on the table.

He fell to his knees, pressing his full weight against the bar, rolling it back inch by inch until the flashlight revealed a tiny finger hole. But the boy had no sooner started to lift the secret door when they heard a strange rustling sound outside and Nancy switched off her light.

At this moment, Mr. Drew and Nancy's friends were still talking and had decided, for the time being, not to hire a boat for Murano.

"Did Nancy say how long they expected to be gone?" her father inquired.

"No," George said, "but based on our trip there today, I'd say no more than two or three hours. She asked us not to call the police till morning, though, if we didn't hear from them."

"That's too long to suit me," Mr. Drew said. "But let's wait a bit longer before we plunge ahead. So long as Ned is with Nancy and they have a boat and a driver at their disposal, I'm sure Ned will head her back if the going gets too rough."

Despite all of his assurances, his listeners doubted that Ned could succeed in changing Nancy's mind once she was on the track of something important.

"Sir," Dave said, changing the subject, "you started to tell us about your client. Did you say he's in the glass business?"

"That's right," the man replied, sitting back on the bench and gazing at the lagoon. "But it seems he's gotten mixed up with some unscrupulous people over here who have accused him of stealing their designs. It's absolutely ridiculous—"

"Why do you say that?" Bess asked.

"Because I know my client. He's impulsive and enthusiastic, but he's not a thief." Mr. Drew paused before he continued his story. "On Giorgio's last trip to Rome, the Italians gave him some dishware to show his sales people in the States. He asked me what I thought of his going into partnership with the Italian factory, and I said I wasn't in favor of it, mostly because of his own particular business problems.

"Unfortunately, Giorgio had already made his decision. He had started negotiations anyway, and they fell through. That didn't surprise me completely—"

"But I still don't understand why the factory people say he's a thief," Burt interrupted.

"Well, because in the midst of their talks, the designs started turning up on dishes sold in the States," the lawyer replied grimly.

"Maybe someone who works for him made a dishonest deal for himself," Dave suggested.

"Quite possible," Mr. Drew said, "but I have a hunch that the Italian factory had a hand in it."

"Why would the factory try to frame Giorgio, though?" George asked.

"To take over his business ultimately. They're threatening to sue him for a lot of money—money he doesn't have. It's all tied up in his company."

"How terrible," the cousins murmured almost in unison.

"What are you going to do, Mr. Drew?" Bess added.

"I'm not sure exactly. I'd like to meet Mr. Alberini. He's one of the owners of the Italian firm. If he's not available, I'll try to see Mr. Scarpa."

"Did you say Scarpa?" Bess blurted out. "Is his first name Erminio?"

19

Taking a Risk

Carson Drew stared blankly into the expectant faces of his listeners, wondering why there was so much intense interest in his response. "Erminio Scarpa?" he repeated. "Come to think of it, I don't remember his first name offhand. It's among my papers, I'm sure. But tell me about the man you mentioned."

That was all the prompting Bess needed. She and George described their encounter with the night clerk, mostly emphasizing his insistence about accompanying Bess to the basilica.

"He and his cohorts just wanted to keep Nancy, George, and me out of their hair," Bess concluded.

As the discussion wore on, Nancy's father became increasingly agitated. He asked several questions about the trip to Murano, finally proposing that they acquire a boat. "Or better yet a police escort," he said. "I noticed a phone on the street for just such emergencies, so if you'll excuse me a moment—"

"We'll wait right here," George said, watching him disappear under the arcade toward the darkened street.

"Nancy will have our hides for this," Bess said to the others, even though she was sure their course of action was the right one.

She had no idea that, only minutes before, the young detective and Ned had crawled under the long worktable in the glassmakers' supply room, listening to the rustle of leaves outside in the still night air.

"Someone's out there," Nancy whispered to the boy.

"Maybe more than one person," he added.

The couple lapsed into silence as the factory door swung open, admitting a flash of light that streamed across the floor to the kilns and crates of broken glass where it stopped. Then the light moved again and the two detectives heard more than one pair of footsteps.

"Just as I thought," Ned murmured, while Nancy leaned forward to follow the traveling light through the small window. "They'll see you," her friend warned and drew the girl back.

Now the steps shuffled closer to the storeroom door, and the handle turned back and forth, causing Ned's heart to thump high in his throat.

Good thing I locked it again, Nancy thought. But what if those men have a key?

She held her breath, praying for the handle to stop moving. Then, to her relief, it did; and she felt Ned relax beside her as he put a hand on her arm. The men, moreover, had begun to talk in a normal, conversational tone.

Too bad I didn't take a course in Italian before I came here! Ned chided himself.

Nancy, on the other hand, concentrated hard on the words and, catching a few of them that she understood, was able to construe the discussion.

They don't have a key for the storeroom door, she gathered. Someone else does. Someone named Alberini.

Then, before she could discern the rest of what was said, the men moved toward the window. They peered inside, exploring the table with the flashlight and, in its beam, picked up the hinged side of the trapdoor. The other end, from which the bar had been removed, stayed hidden under the broad darkness of the table.

Thank goodness, Nancy said to herself, now following the cone of light to the sacks of potash that stood nearby. Suddenly, she heard her name.

"Nancy Drew," one man had said unmistakably, among other words spoken in angry tones. A shiver of fright coursed through his listeners as he pounded his fist once on the small window. Had he seen them after all?

No, he's only trying to vent his frustration, the girl concluded, because if he knew for a fact we were in here, he'd break the glass!

That thought, however, had not occurred to Ned, who was prepared to tackle either of the men if they so much as stepped inside the storeroom. But at last they left the factory.

"Come on, Ned," Nancy said, sliding out of their hiding place. "I want to see what's below this floor."

"You know something?" Ned replied with a soft chuckle. "You really are amazing. My heart stopped beating about five minutes ago, and you're ready to plunge right in again."

"And to think I believed your heart never stopped beating for me," the young detective said lightly. "Come on."

She focused the small flashlight on the finger hole that Ned pulled back on. "It's stuck," he said, pretending it wouldn't budge.

"What?" Nancy gasped, disappointed; but seeing the grin on her friend's face, she realized he was only joking.

He swung the panel wide, revealing a ladder that stretched beyond the dimming glow of Nancy's flashlight to a room bathed in blackness.

"I'm afraid the batteries are ready to give out," she admitted sheepishly, "so I'd better try to save them."

She flicked off the light once she had a firm foothold on the ladder and began to descend slowly, causing the boy to follow with equal caution. When they reached the bottom, Nancy turned the light on again, directing it to a full-length mirror that was obviously undergoing restoration.

But besides seeing her image and that of Ned's, she noticed a canvas sack heaped over something. A white lacy collar surfaced in the light. Instantly, the girl detective turned, letting the beam fall directly on the heavy cloth. It was covering the inert form of the *duchessa*!

"Oh!" Nancy cried, running toward the woman, who appeared to be asleep.

"She's alive, isn't she?" Ned asked anxiously while his companion touched the figure. There was no reaction, however.

"Yes, but I think she's been drugged, Ned."

As she spoke, the *duchessa* let out a soft, pitiful cry much like that of a whimpering puppy. Ned lifted her frail body and carried it to the ladder.

Then, sighing, he realized that he would be unable to take the woman upstairs unless he put her over his shoulder, and even that would be risky given the narrowness of the opening overhead.

"I think we have a problem," he told Nancy, and pointed to their escape hatch.

"You're right," she said, but could not come up with a solution.

"Maybe you or I ought to climb up and tell

the boatman to get the police," Ned suggested.

"But what if somebody catches us leaving?" Nancy responded, suddenly aware of the *duchessa*'s eyes, which had begun to open ever so slightly. "Ned, put her down in that chair over there," she said.

He did, and Nancy curled her arm gently around the woman's shoulder. "Who brought you here?" she asked.

Maria Dandolo said something in Italian, then as if suddenly aware she had been addressed in English, she translated her words, weakly but with clarity.

"Two men."

"What are their names?" Nancy pressed her.

"Alberini and—Scarpa."

"Did they tell you where your nephew Filippo is?" the girl continued.

"Oh, no—poor Filippo." The woman moaned and began to weep piteously. "No—don't hurt him," she pleaded.

"*Duchessa*, do you know where he is?" Nancy repeated with an intensity and firmness that ended the crying.

"No. Anyway, I wouldn't believe whatever Mr. Alberini said."

There was another long, intolerable pause that made Nancy wonder if the woman had somehow hidden the answer in the recesses of her mind, vehemently refusing to accept it.

"Oh, please, *Duchessa*, it's very important that you tell me. I want to help you," Nancy said slowly. "I want to find Filippo."

But again the woman moaned uncontrollably.

"It's no use, Ned," Nancy remarked in despair.

"Well, just tell me what you want to do. Other than my original idea, I can't think of a thing."

Nancy, however, began questioning the *duchessa* once more.

"Are the men going to take you to see your nephew?" she asked.

"They promised me they would if—"

"If what?" the young detective prompted her.

"If I give them the formula."

"Is that why you came here to the factory in the first place?"

"Yes."

Nancy then recalled the seeming intrusion at the woman's apartment on San Gregorio. Papers had been pulled from the desk and strewn everywhere. Had Nancy's first deduction been wrong about an intruder? Wasn't it more likely that the *duchessa* had finally succumbed to the kidnappers' threats and searched frantically for her own copy of the formula?

When she didn't find it she came to Murano! Nancy thought. "What happened to your own copy of the formula?" she blurted out to Ned's surprise.

"I don't know. I could not find it in my desk."

"Did you find another copy?" the young detective went on. "Here, in the storage room, I mean."

"No."

Nancy sipped in another long breath. "Did the men say they'd be back to see you?"

"Yes," the *duchessa* said, her voice now almost inaudible. "Then—they made me call you. They said they would harm Filippo if I refused. I'm sorry, Nancy—so—sorry—" With that, she sank back exhausted and inert once again.

"Pretty clever plan," Nancy said. "Our two friends probably expected to catch me on their second visit. Perhaps I shouldn't disappoint them!"

20

Venetian Victory

Ned stared at Nancy in utter surprise. "Are you serious?"

"Yes, I am," the young detective replied. "You see, if I stall them long enough, you'll have time to get help."

"And you expect me to leave you on this island alone—without me to protect you?"

"Look, Ned, it's our only chance to find out where Filippo is," Nancy insisted. "The minute you get back to Venice—"

"Why don't I stay here," Ned cut in, "and send the boatman for help?"

"I don't know if we can rely on him. Besides

if the police doubt his story, he may not persist enough to convince them."

"What'll we do with the *duchessa*?"

"We'll have to leave her here for the time being. Ned, please, it's the only way. Believe me!" Nancy urged.

"Whatever you say," Ned replied in a quiet voice.

"I'll keep the men talking as long as I can," the girl said, pulling a small brush from her handbag. She worked the dark powder out of her hair and wiped off her makeup with a handkerchief before scurrying up the ladder.

"Be careful," Ned said anxiously.

"I will. I promise. Now please, don't worry."

Easier said than done, the boy thought, but he lay the *duchessa* on the floor again and prepared for his own departure while Nancy slipped out of the building and onto the grassy walkway that led to the showroom. She slowed her pace only a moment when she heard Ned's feet on the pavement going in the opposite direction toward the dock, then sped forward again.

Upon reaching the showroom entrance, however, she did not ring the bell but stepped softly inside, the thick carpet shielding her from detection.

They must be upstairs, she decided and climbed to the landing.

To her surprise, all doors on the second floor were locked. Men's voices, however, came from one room. They were muffled by the separation of the wall, but as the young detective listened, she realized there were four people speaking in English. One of them was an American. The second was the manager of the glass factory, Mr. Chiais, and the third, Erminio Scarpa!

"Now, Erminio, this is Beppe Alberini talking to you as a friend," the American said, but his words were cut short by a disbelieving laugh—Scarpa's, Nancy surmised.

"You have nothing to worry about," Alberini continued. "So long as the other clerk was willing to give you an alibi, no one will believe some stupid amateur detective."

"But her friend—the one I took to the basilica—she can identify me; and Lucia says Nancy Drew knows where we live."

"But you and Francesco will be out of the country before we get caught. We'll see to it."

"That's right," the manager said. "As soon as we get what we want from Signore Dandolo—"

He's talking about the formula, Nancy thought.

"—we'll join you. It's all very simple," Chiais finished. "Don't worry about the girl. She is only a nuisance, nothing more dangerous than that."

Nancy felt her skin tingle in disgust as the conversation continued. The fourth man in the room, she found out, was Scarpa's brother Francesco, who was in business with Alberini; and it was he, Alberini, and Erminio who had tried to kidnap Filippo's father. But when they couldn't find him, they took Filippo instead. Their plan was to ruin the Dandolo business. After that, they would take care of a contact in the United States by the name of Giorgio, a man whom they had induced into partnership.

It sounds as if they want to create their own little monopoly, Nancy thought, and push all the competition out by any means possible.

When the men started to talk about more casual matters that were of no further interest to the young detective, she knocked firmly on the door.

A chair slid back in response, and Beppe Alberini snarled, "Who's there?"

"Nancy Drew," the girl said cheerfully. "I'm looking for the *duchessa*."

"Ah, yes, of course," the man replied and opened the door. He had a round face, balding black hair and a sarcastic smile on his lips as he pulled Nancy inside. "You know these gentlemen, I believe."

Nancy nodded even though she had never met Francesco Scarpa before. "I would like to see the *duchessa*, please."

"In a moment," Alberini said. "First, I'd like to know how much you have been able to figure out about our operation."

The girl's mind raced. Should she tell the men what she knew? Perhaps it was better not to, yet it might be the only way to stall them!

"Well, I know one of you broke into the Artistico Vetro showroom on the night of our arrival in Venice," she began. Then she voiced a hunch she had had all along. "Since nothing was stolen, although a chandelier fell off the ceiling, I suppose your purpose was to bug the *duchessa*'s apartment."

"*Brava*!" Alberini exclaimed. "You are, indeed, a clever girl."

"Who did it?" Nancy inquired, but when no one responded. she answered her own question. "I would say Erminio Scarpa. Now I'm sure you're wondering how I figured that out."

She watched the men's rapt faces, stringing out her words slowly. "When Mr. Scarpa came to our room later that night, I noticed that the bottoms of his pants legs were wet." Now Nancy turned to the night clerk. "You pulled that little job, didn't you, just before you came on duty at the hotel? Your boat must've been leaking just enough to leave those telltale wet marks on your trousers."

Furious, the man glared at her but did not speak.

"You were probably the one who also tried to push me off the *vaporetto* the next day," Nancy accused him.

Alberini smiled. "A young lady with your brains and good looks would be an asset to our company. Perhaps, when we're all finished here, we'll offer you a job."

"Thank you, but no thanks," Nancy said coldly. She stared at the man with disgust, then let her eyes roam across the room. They settled on a cap hanging on a coatrack. It was similar to the one Ned had found on the bridge near the Hotel Excelsior after the boys' boat had been attacked.

"Who's cap is this?" she asked, walking toward it.

"Mine," Alberini said. "Why?"

It's quite new, isn't it?" Nancy went on. "You bought it after you lost your other one when you did your rope trick at the bridge, trying to sink my friends' boat."

Alberini's lips spread into an evil grin. "So you found my other one, eh? I'll be glad to take it back. I can always use two."

Where you're going you won't need any, Nancy said to herself, adding aloud, "We've also figured out that it was Erminio Scarpa who went through the other hotel room—the one my Emerson friends were staying in."

"Yes, he was looking for something that belonged to us," Alberini admitted.

"Was it a beautiful glass horse, perchance?"

"Obviously. Francesco had flown to Vienna to sell it to a prospective customer, but unfortunately the deal fell through. He couldn't very well leave it aboard his plane but naturally he was afraid to bring it back through customs since he assumed the officials had been alerted. So he planted it in the boy's suitcase."

"He must've overheard Ned say he and his friends planned to stay at the Gritti Palace Hotel," Nancy put in.

"Exactly, Miss Drew. And since Erminio had access to the rooms there, it would be easy enough to retrieve the statue, or so he thought. By the way, what did your friends do with it?"

"The customs people broke it by accident."

"Oh, what a shame, and it was such a lovely piece, worth quite a bit of money, too." Alberini sighed.

"One thing puzzles me," Nancy addressed the hotel clerk. She riveted her eyes on his. "You probably knew the boys had been arrested and you must've realized that the police wouldn't have permitted them to leave with an expensive glass sculpture that they had allegedly smuggled into the country. So—why did you bother looking for it?"

"Because Alberini told me that he had fixed it with the police to let the boys keep the piece. He said he paid off the captain—" Scarpa's words faded as he stared at his accomplice. "Why did you tell me that?"

"I know why," Nancy said. "Because he wanted you to steal the statue from Ned's room and then have *you* arrested for it. It was a frame-up to get you out of the picture. He probably intended to get rid of your brother as well by a similar scheme.

Now it was Francesco Scarpa's turn to glare at Alberini. "Why, you double-crossing—" he roared. "You lied to us!" A string of Italian utterances spewed angrily from his mouth until he swallowed hard and stopped. "Oh, why did we ever listen to you? You even fooled Lucia and Antonella."

Antonella, Nancy thought, must be his younger sister. "I saw Antonella's photograph," she said, hoping to bring the *duchessa*'s nephew back into the conversation. "She was standing next to Filippo Dandolo."

"It was through her that we were able to persuade Filippo to do some designs for us," Erminio Scarpa said. "It was all Beppe's idea. He gave the designs to an American business associate. He wanted to expand his operation to the United States."

"Shut up!" Alberini hissed, "or we'll all end up in jail. Let's silence this little busybody and get out of here before her friends alert the police!"

But he had barely finished his sentence when a flurry of noise stirred outside. Then the door flung open and a team of uniformed officers, followed by Mr. Drew and Nancy's friends, dashed forward.

"Dad!" the girl cried, running into his arms as Ned and the others circled her. "Oh, I'm so glad to see you!"

"I hope we didn't interrupt an interesting conversation." Her father grinned.

"Not at all. The interesting part just finished. They were about to get rid of me, and I think they meant for good!" Nancy said, as Ned pinched his eyes in worry.

"I knew this plan of yours was risky!" he said.

"But it worked, didn't it?" Nancy exclaimed jubilantly. "I can tell you their entire scheme—everything!"

Mr. Drew, however, held up a hand. "Before you do, there are a few other people who would like to hear it, I'm sure," he said.

A moment later, Andreoli stepped into the room followed by another police officer and the *duchessa*.

"Oh, *Duchessa*!" Nancy exclaimed, hugging her and helping her to a chair.

"I'm afraid I wasn't too coherent before, was I, my dear?"

"Nonsense," the girl said.

"That's kind of you to say," the woman said, sinking back wearily. "But the drugs seem to have worn off now and I should be able to understand everything much better. First, I want to thank you, Nancy. You saved my life, you know!"

Nancy did not reply, however, as she lit on Ned's gaze. "I'm not sure your life really was in danger—"

"But it was," Andreoli insisted in perfect English. "You see, my sister is not very strong, and another night in that awful, damp cellar would have been detrimental to her health."

"Your sister?" Nancy and her friends repeated, gaping at him.

"Yes. You see, I'm Filippo's father."

"What?" Bess cried, as the man pulled off the black beard he had worn, now revealing the distinguished face of a man in his early sixties.

"I put this on so no one would recognize me. Only Maria knew of my disguise."

"But when she asked us to help her, why didn't you tell us?" George inquired.

"I was afraid to. Suppose you had fallen into the hands of our adversaries? They could have pried the information out of you."

"It's not that we didn't trust you," Maria Dandolo interjected. "We simply felt it wasn't essential for you to know where Claudio was, and we wanted to avoid even the slightest slip on anyone's part."

Then, she turned to the manager. "I had no idea, Giuseppe, that you were part of all this. How very sad. How very, very sad indeed."

Her listener merely looked away, unable to respond.

"And now, where is Filippo?" Signore Dandolo asked at last. He fired an angered glare at the men who remained defiantly closemouthed until Erminio Scarpa spoke.

"What's the use?" he said, coughing out the answer. "He's on Torcello, in a room behind the museum there."

"Opposite Santa Maria Assunta? Yes, I know

it well There is a stone on the wall that bears the winged lion. I can still see Filippo's face when I took him to the island as a small boy. He loved it so, and I believe that was what he had in mind when he adopted the symbol as his artist's signature."

Instantly, the police captain ordered some of his men to the island.

"Before we leave," Mr. Drew said, "I have a question for Francesco Scarpa. Just what is your connection with my client, Giorgio?"

The man scowled. "You figure it out."

"I think I already have," the attorney replied. "You planned to push Giorgio out of a very successful business by accusing him of stealing designs that you forced Filippo to create under threats of harm to the rest of his family. You showed the designs to Giorgio and his sales people, then gave them to another American manufacturer who began to mass market them. Correct?"

Erminio's brother did not answer.

"That was all he and Alberini needed to start a lawsuit," Burt added.

"Actually," Mr. Drew continued, "they had no intention of going through with it. That's why I got no action from the lawyer in Rome and why Giorgio sent me over here to look into things."

"But then what were they after if not damages from a lawsuit?" Bess asked.

"A settlement."

"And don't forget Giorgio's business!" Dave concluded.

"With the Dandolo formula in hand, they could double it quickly and successfully all over the world," Nancy observed.

"By the way, where is the formula, *signore*?" Ned asked Filippo's father. "Safe and sound, I hope."

"It's right here," the man said, tapping his forehead. "I destroyed all the written copies, even my sister's, just to make sure no one could possibly get hold of it. Unfortunately, she left for Murano before I could tell her what I had done."

"I—I could not stand the pressure and the threats any longer," the woman admitted. "I feared for Filippo's life, which, for both of us, is worth much more than anything else in the world. You understand that, Claudio, don't you?"

"Of course I do," the *signore* said gently.

"Were the men at your apartment when I called you yesterday and you said you needed not only me?" Nancy asked the *duchessa*.

"Yes. That's when I was going through my desk looking for the formula. When I couldn't find it, they brought me here."

"We came to the factory this afternoon," Nancy said. "I saw someone in the inner storeroom who resembled you. Was it you?"

The woman closed her eyes for a moment. "I tried to get to the window to attract your attention, but the men pulled me away and out of sight before I succeeded."

Now, as the prisoners departed, Nancy wondered whether her next mystery would pose as much of a challenge as the one she had encountered in Italy. She would find out very soon when she found herself caught in a *Race Against Time*.

Meanwhile, though, she was more than happy to see Filippo reunited with his family. He proved to be an attractive young man in his thirties with sparkling eyes that betrayed his sense of humor.

Later that evening when everyone gathered for their last dinner in Venice, Nancy presented one question that only Filippo could answer.

"How did you manage to send the note with the winged lion on it to your aunt?" she asked.

"Before they took me away, I heard one of the men say we were going to Torcello," the young man said. "I had a piece of paper in my jacket and I always carry pencils in my shirt pocket. So I quickly scribbled the note and Aunt Maria's address and dropped it on the street. Apparently someone found it and delivered it to the house."

"That was clever of you, Filippo," George complimented him.

"I wanted to write a message, but as you can imagine, I didn't have time. Once I had put down the address and the symbol, I realized the men were watching me. I told them I had an idea for a new design and stuck the paper back in my pocket for a second. Then, when they weren't looking, I pulled it out and dropped it."

"Unfortunately, neither I nor Claudio connected the message with Torcello," the *duchessa* said, chiding herself.

"Now, now," Filippo said, "let's not talk

about all this unpleasantness anymore. Especially since this dinner is really in honor of my favorite detective."

"Only one detective?" his aunt asked brightly. "I count six of them!"

"Well, my dear aunt, I intend to make five more of these, if you'll all accept them?"

"Oh, my goodness. How wonderful!" Bess cried, watching the veil of gauze fall away from a magnificent glass etching.

On it was the artist's famed signature—a large winged lion—and underneath the words, *My most grateful thanks to Nancy Drew.*

"And ours, too," the *duchessa* said on behalf of herself and Filippo's father.

"This really belongs to all of you," Nancy told her friends, rising to accept the gift.

"Don't worry, don't worry! I said I will make more! A hundred of them, if you like!" Filippo exclaimed, bringing a round of applause and laughter.